DISNEY
FROZEN

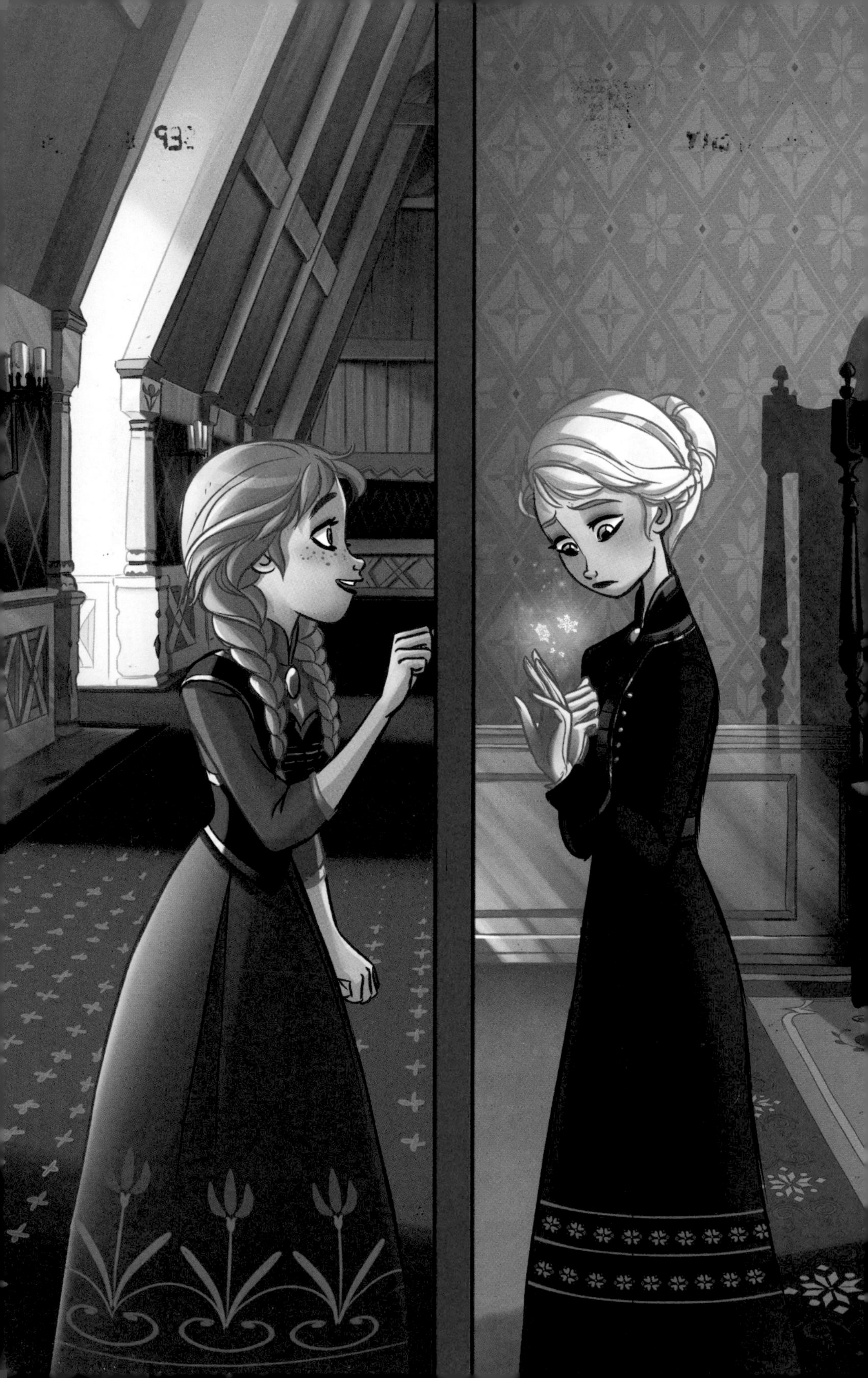

DISNEY FROZEN

SCRIPT BY **CECIL CASTELLUCCI**

LINE ART BY **PAOLA ANTISTA**

COLORING BY **FRANCESCA CAROTENUTO** AND
WES DZIOBA

LETTERING BY **RICHARD STARKINGS** AND
COMICRAFT'S JIMMY BETANCOURT

COVER ART BY **PAOLA ANTISTA** WITH
FRANCESCA CAROTENUTO

DARK HORSE BOOKS

DARK HORSE BOOKS

PRESIDENT AND PUBLISHER
MIKE RICHARDSON

EDITOR
FREDDYE MILLER

ASSISTANT EDITOR
JUDY KHUU

DESIGNER
CINDY CACEREZ-SPRAGUE

DIGITAL ART TECHNICIAN
SAMANTHA HUMMER

NEIL HANKERSON EXECUTIVE VICE PRESIDENT TOM WEDDLE CHIEF FINANCIAL OFFICER RANDY STRADLEY VICE PRESIDENT OF PUBLISHING NICK McWHORTER CHIEF BUSINESS DEVELOPMENT OFFICER DALE LaFOUNTAIN CHIEF INFORMATION OFFICER MATT PARKINSON VICE PRESIDENT OF MARKETING CARA NIECE VICE PRESIDENT OF PRODUCTION AND SCHEDULING MARK BERNARDI VICE PRESIDENT OF BOOK TRADE AND DIGITAL SALES KEN LIZZI GENERAL COUNSEL DAVE MARSHALL EDITOR IN CHIEF DAVEY ESTRADA EDITORIAL DIRECTOR CHRIS WARNER SENIOR BOOKS EDITOR CARY GRAZZINI DIRECTOR OF SPECIALTY PROJECTS LIA RIBACCHI ART DIRECTOR VANESSA TODD-HOLMES DIRECTOR OF PRINT PURCHASING MATT DRYER DIRECTOR OF DIGITAL ART AND PREPRESS MICHAEL GOMBOS SENIOR DIRECTOR OF LICENSED PUBLICATIONS KARI YADRO DIRECTOR OF CUSTOM PROGRAMS KARI TORSON DIRECTOR OF INTERNATIONAL LICENSING SEAN BRICE DIRECTOR OF TRADE SALES

DISNEY PUBLISHING WORLDWIDE GLOBAL MAGAZINES, COMICS AND PARTWORKS PUBLISHER Lynn Waggoner • EDITORIAL TEAM Bianca Coletti (Director, Magazines), Guido Frazzini (Director, Comics), Carlotta Quattrocolo (Executive Editor), Stefano Ambrosio (Executive Editor, New IP), Camilla Vedove (Senior Manager, Editorial Development), Behnoosh Khalili (Senior Editor), Julie Dorris (Senior Editor), Mina Riazi (Assistant Editor), Gabriela Capasso (Assistant Editor) • DESIGN Enrico Soave (Senior Designer) • ART Ken Shue (VP, Global Art), Manny Mederos (Senior Illustration Manager, Comics and Magazines), Roberto Santillo (Creative Director), Marco Ghiglione (Creative Manager), Stefano Attardi (Illustration Manager) • PORTFOLIO MANAGEMENT Olivia Ciancarelli (Director) • BUSINESS & MARKETING Mariantonietta Galla (Senior Manager, Franchise), Virpi Korhonen (Editorial Manager)

DISNEY FROZEN

Published by Dark Horse Books
A division of Dark Horse Comics LLC
10956 SE Main Street
Milwaukie, OR 97222

DarkHorse.com

To find a comics shop in your area, visit comicshoplocator.com

First edition: March 2020
ISBN 978-1-50671-403-5
Digital ISBN 978-1-50671-483-7

1 3 5 7 9 10 8 6 4 2
Printed in the United States of America

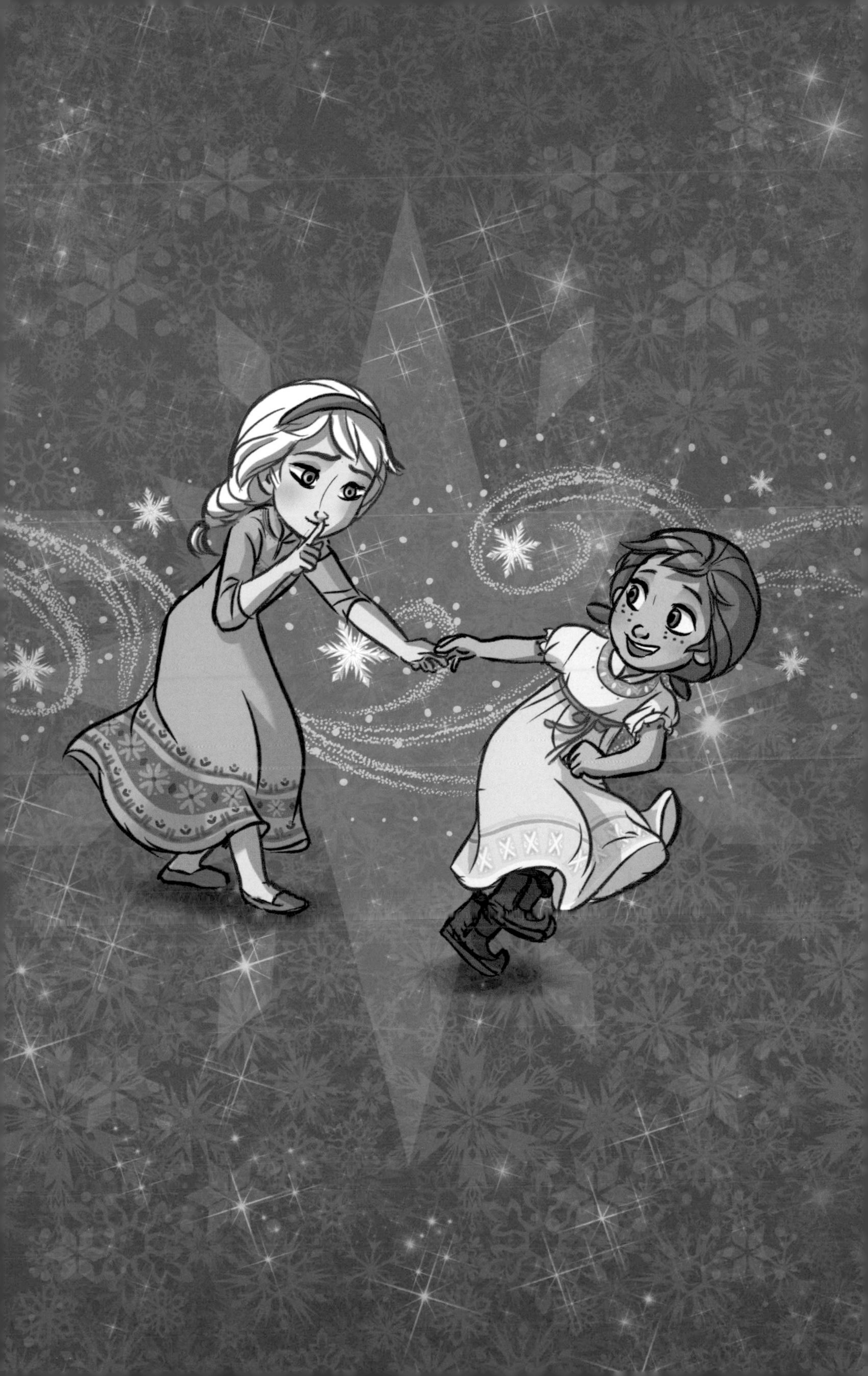

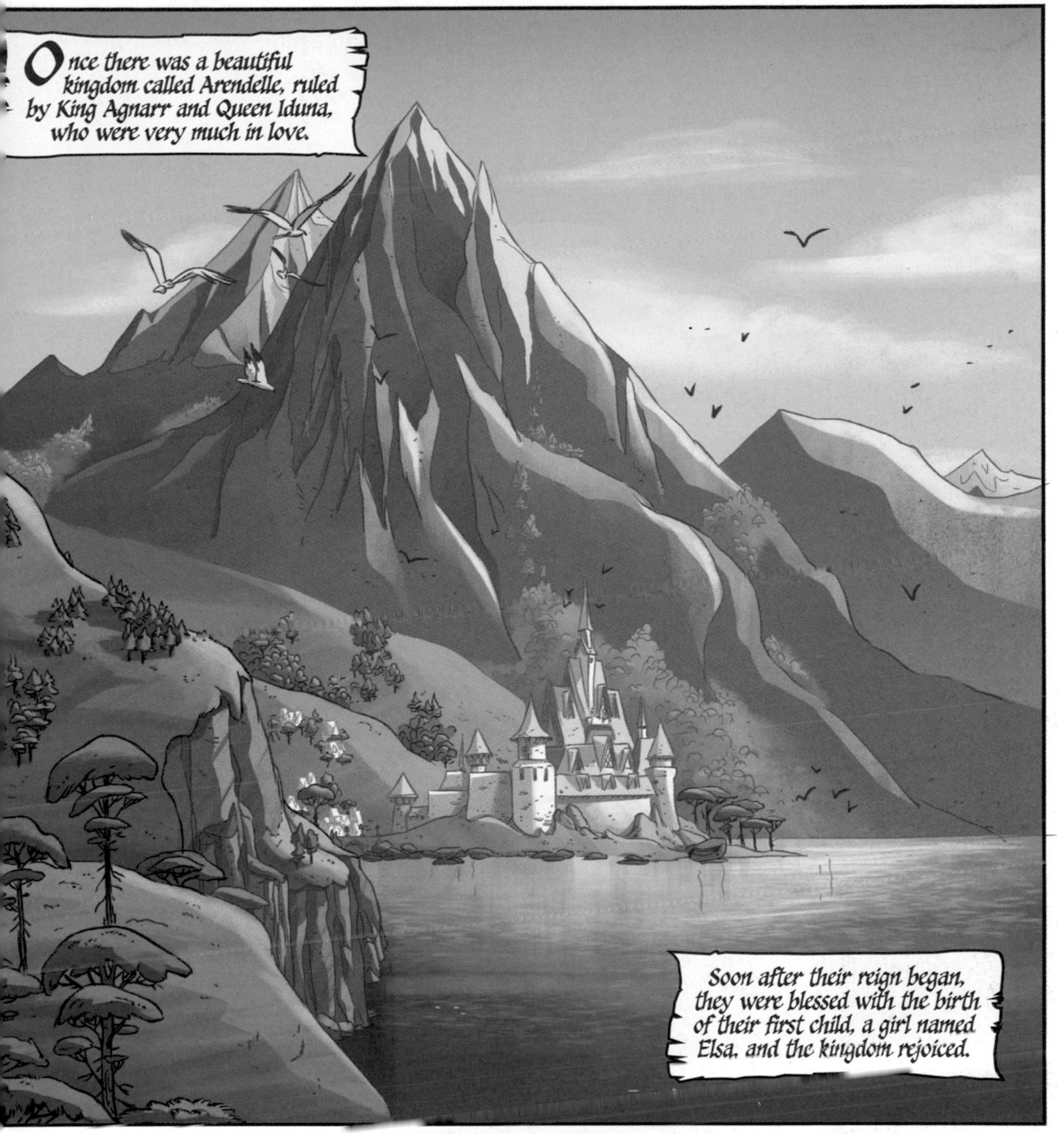
Once there was a beautiful kingdom called Arendelle, ruled by King Agnarr and Queen Iduna, who were very much in love.
Soon after their reign began, they were blessed with the birth of their first child, a girl named Elsa, and the kingdom rejoiced.

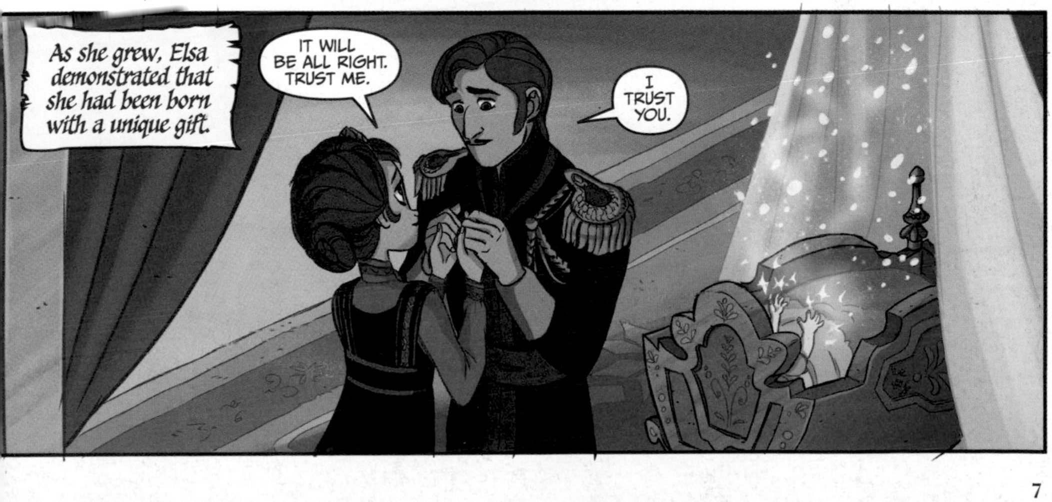
As she grew, Elsa demonstrated that she had been born with a unique gift.
IT WILL BE ALL RIGHT. TRUST ME.
I TRUST YOU.

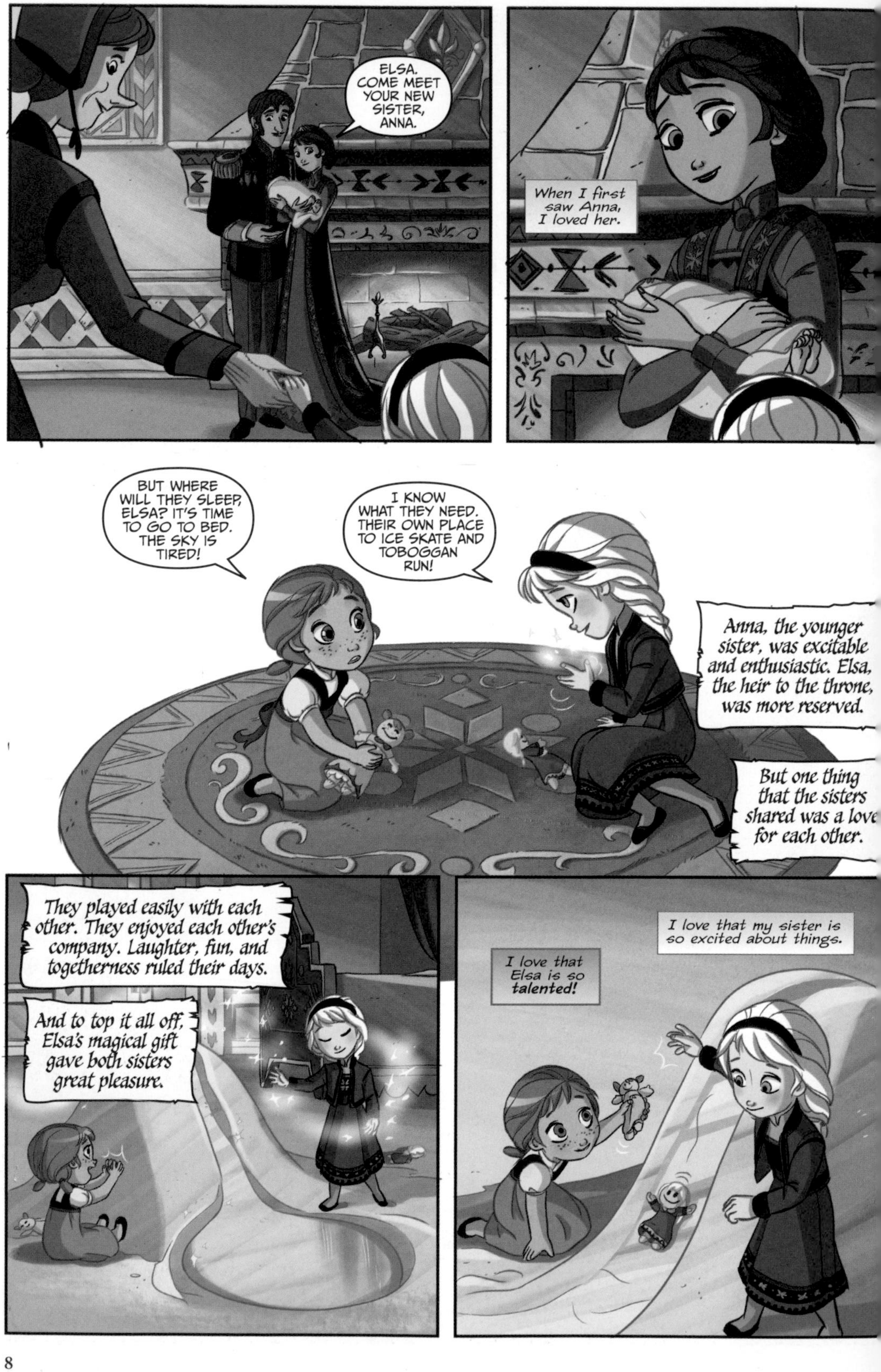
ELSA. COME MEET YOUR NEW SISTER, ANNA.
When I first saw Anna, I loved her.
BUT WHERE WILL THEY SLEEP, ELSA? IT'S TIME TO GO TO BED. THE SKY IS TIRED!
I KNOW WHAT THEY NEED. THEIR OWN PLACE TO ICE SKATE AND TOBOGGAN RUN!
Anna, the younger sister, was excitable and enthusiastic. Elsa, the heir to the throne, was more reserved.
But one thing that the sisters shared was a love for each other.
They played easily with each other. They enjoyed each other's company. Laughter, fun, and togetherness ruled their days.
And to top it all off, Elsa's magical gift gave both sisters great pleasure.
I love that Elsa is so talented!
I love that my sister is so excited about things.

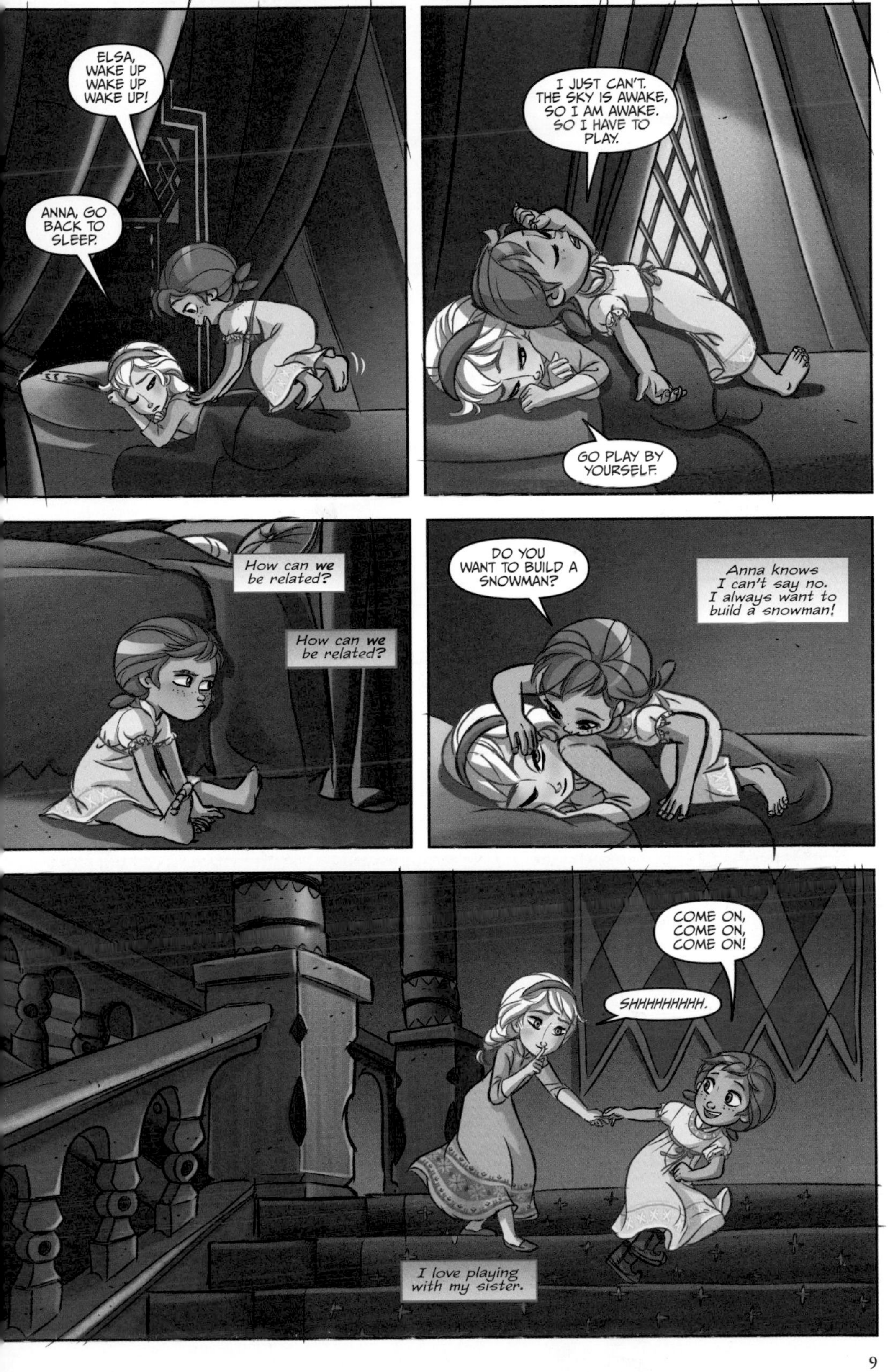
ELSA, WAKE UP WAKE UP WAKE UP!
ANNA, GO BACK TO SLEEP.
I JUST CAN'T. THE SKY IS AWAKE, SO I AM AWAKE. SO I HAVE TO PLAY.
GO PLAY BY YOURSELF.
How can we be related?
How can we be related?
DO YOU WANT TO BUILD A SNOWMAN?
Anna knows I can't say no. I always want to build a snowman!
COME ON, COME ON, COME ON!
SHHHHHHHHH.
I love playing with my sister.

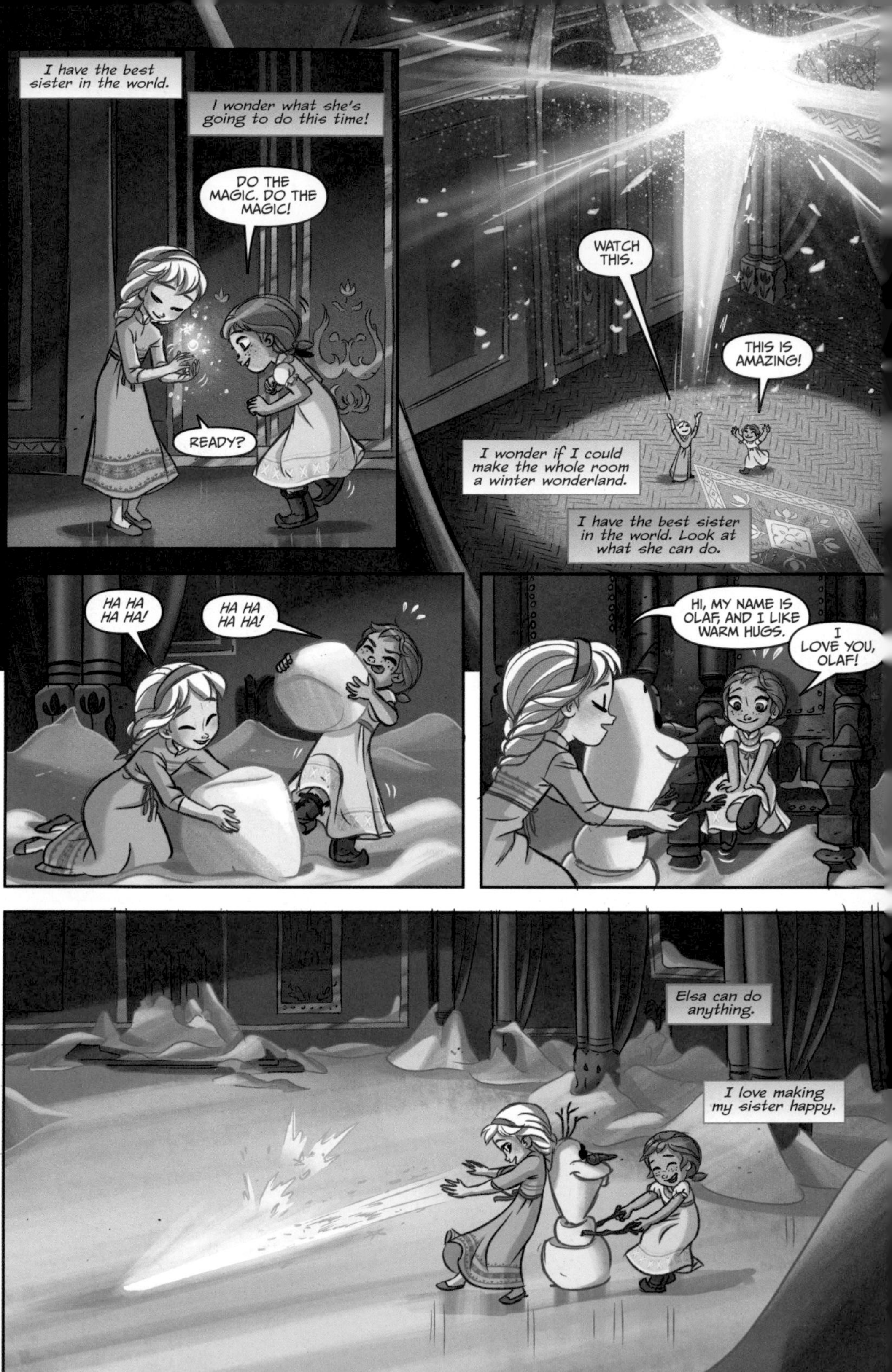
I have the best sister in the world.
I wonder what she's going to do this time!
DO THE MAGIC. DO THE MAGIC!
READY?
WATCH THIS.
THIS IS AMAZING!
I wonder if I could make the whole room a winter wonderland.
I have the best sister in the world. Look at what she can do.
HA HA HA HA!
HA HA HA HA!
HI, MY NAME IS OLAF, AND I LIKE WARM HUGS.
I LOVE YOU, OLAF!
Elsa can do anything.
I love making my sister happy.

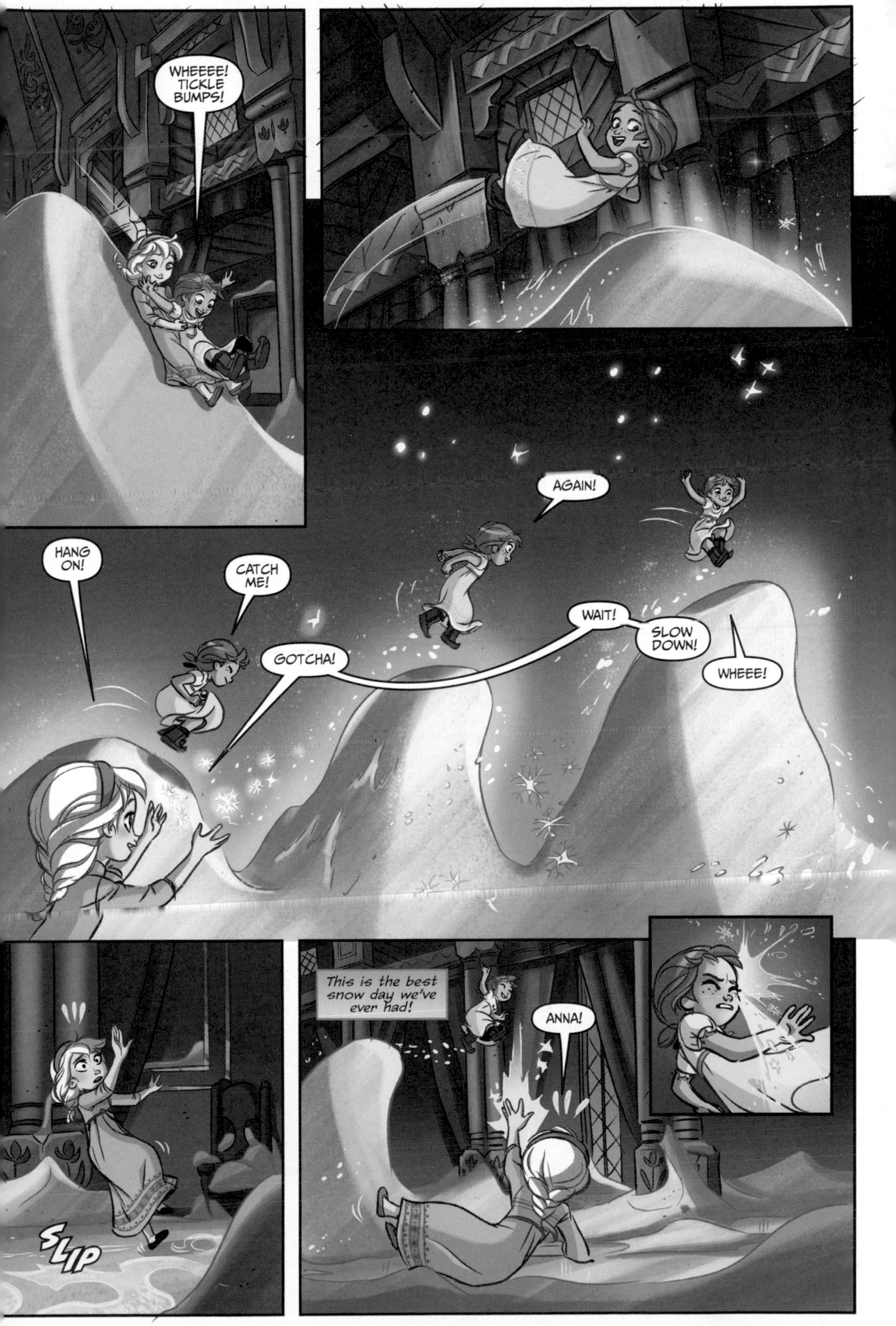

WHEEEE! TICKLE BUMPS!
AGAIN!
HANG ON!
CATCH ME!
GOTCHA!
WAIT!
SLOW DOWN!
WHEEE!
SLIP
This is the best snow day we've ever had!
ANNA!

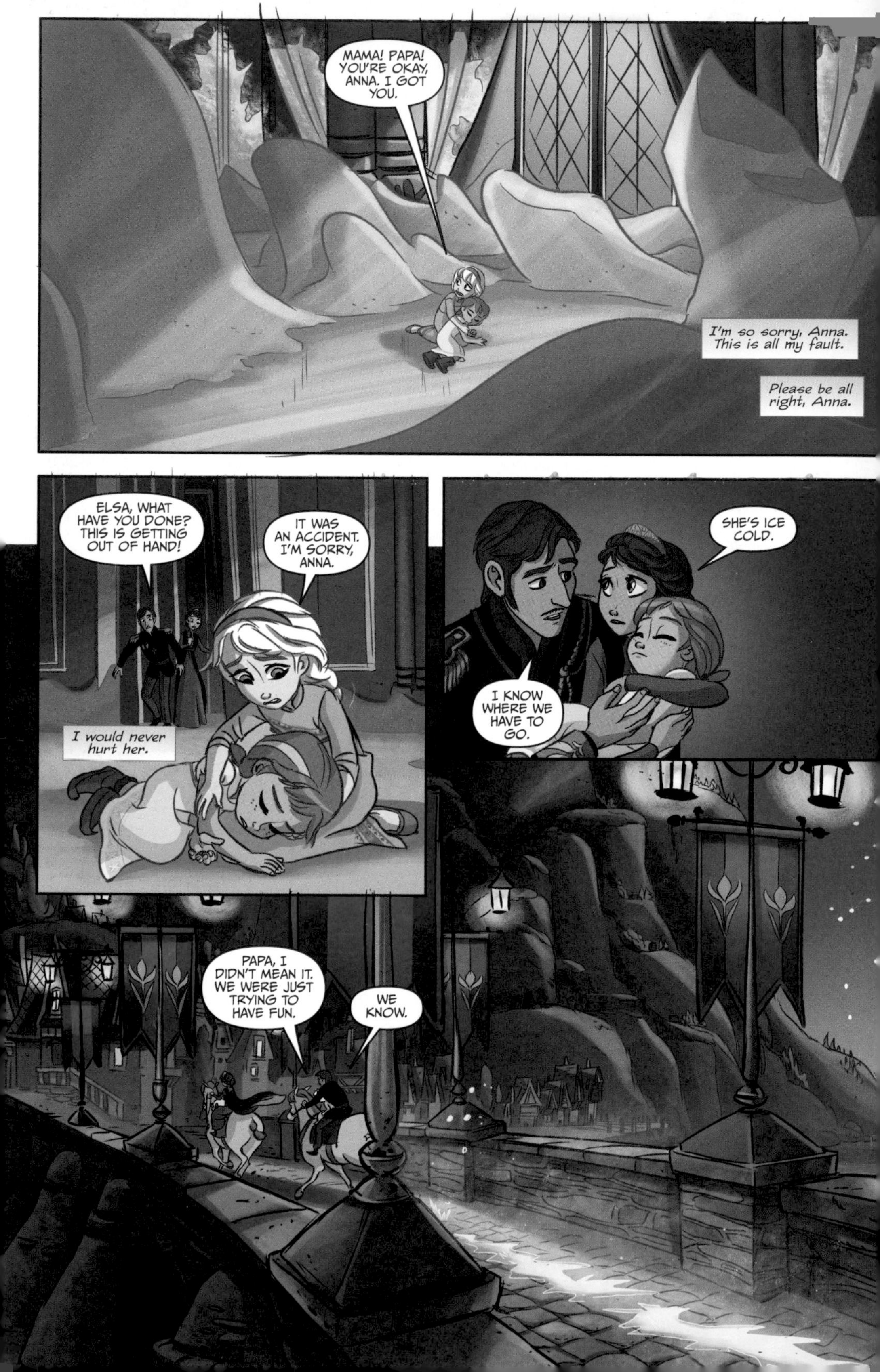
MAMA! PAPA! YOU'RE OKAY, ANNA. I GOT YOU.
I'm so sorry, Anna. This is all my fault.
Please be all right, Anna.
ELSA, WHAT HAVE YOU DONE? THIS IS GETTING OUT OF HAND!
IT WAS AN ACCIDENT. I'M SORRY, ANNA.
I would never hurt her.
SHE'S ICE COLD.
I KNOW WHERE WE HAVE TO GO.
PAPA, I DIDN'T MEAN IT. WE WERE JUST TRYING TO HAVE FUN.
WE KNOW.

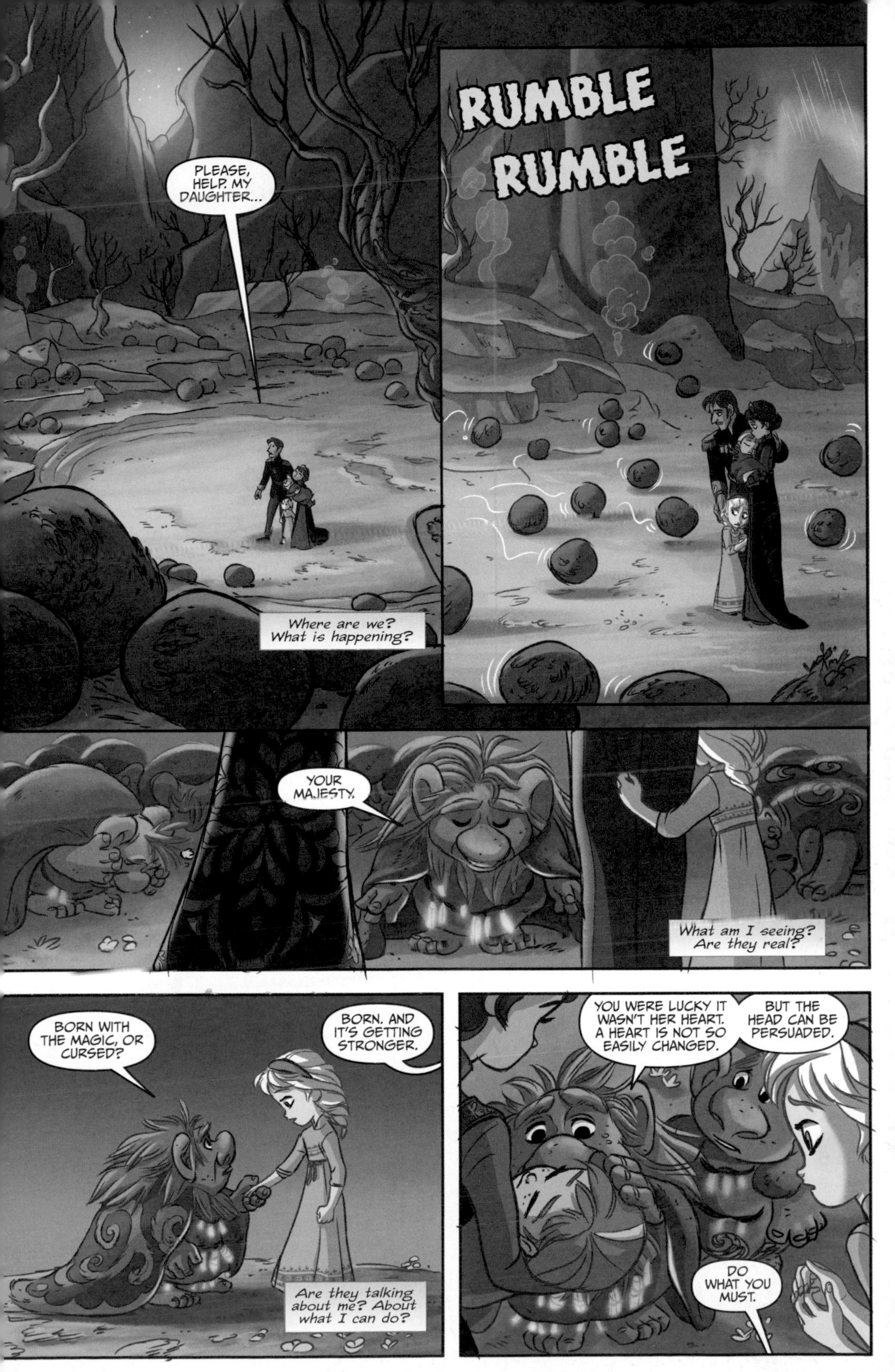
PLEASE, HELP. MY DAUGHTER...
Where are we? What is happening?
RUMBLE RUMBLE
YOUR MAJESTY.
What am I seeing? Are they real?
BORN WITH THE MAGIC, OR CURSED?
BORN. AND IT'S GETTING STRONGER.
Are they talking about me? About what I can do?
YOU WERE LUCKY IT WASN'T HER HEART. A HEART IS NOT SO EASILY CHANGED.
BUT THE HEAD CAN BE PERSUADED.
DO WHAT YOU MUST.

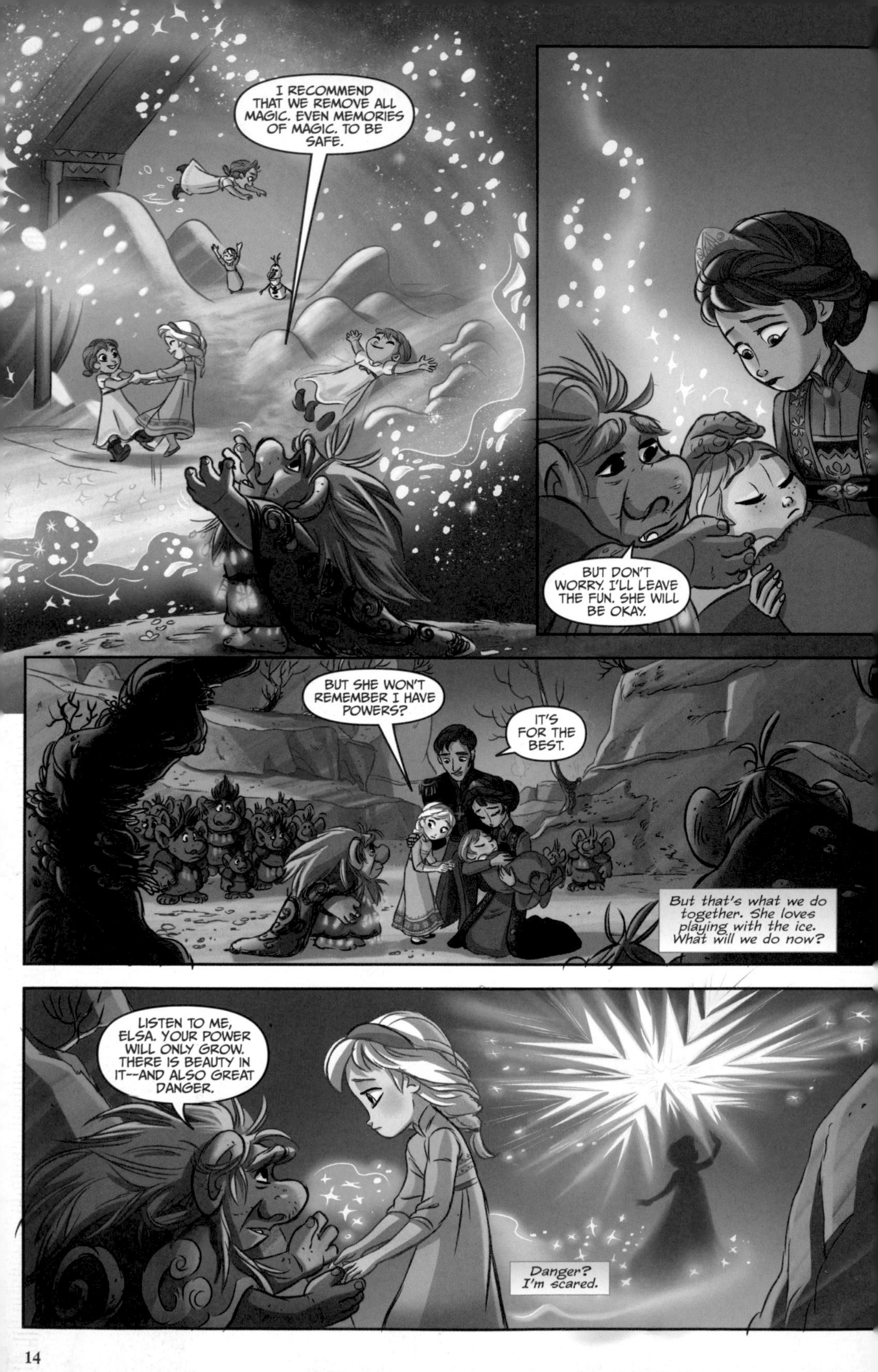
I RECOMMEND THAT WE REMOVE ALL MAGIC. EVEN MEMORIES OF MAGIC. TO BE SAFE.
BUT DON'T WORRY. I'LL LEAVE THE FUN. SHE WILL BE OKAY.
BUT SHE WON'T REMEMBER I HAVE POWERS?
IT'S FOR THE BEST.
But that's what we do together. She loves playing with the ice. What will we do now?
LISTEN TO ME, ELSA. YOUR POWER WILL ONLY GROW. THERE IS BEAUTY IN IT--AND ALSO GREAT DANGER.
Danger? I'm scared.

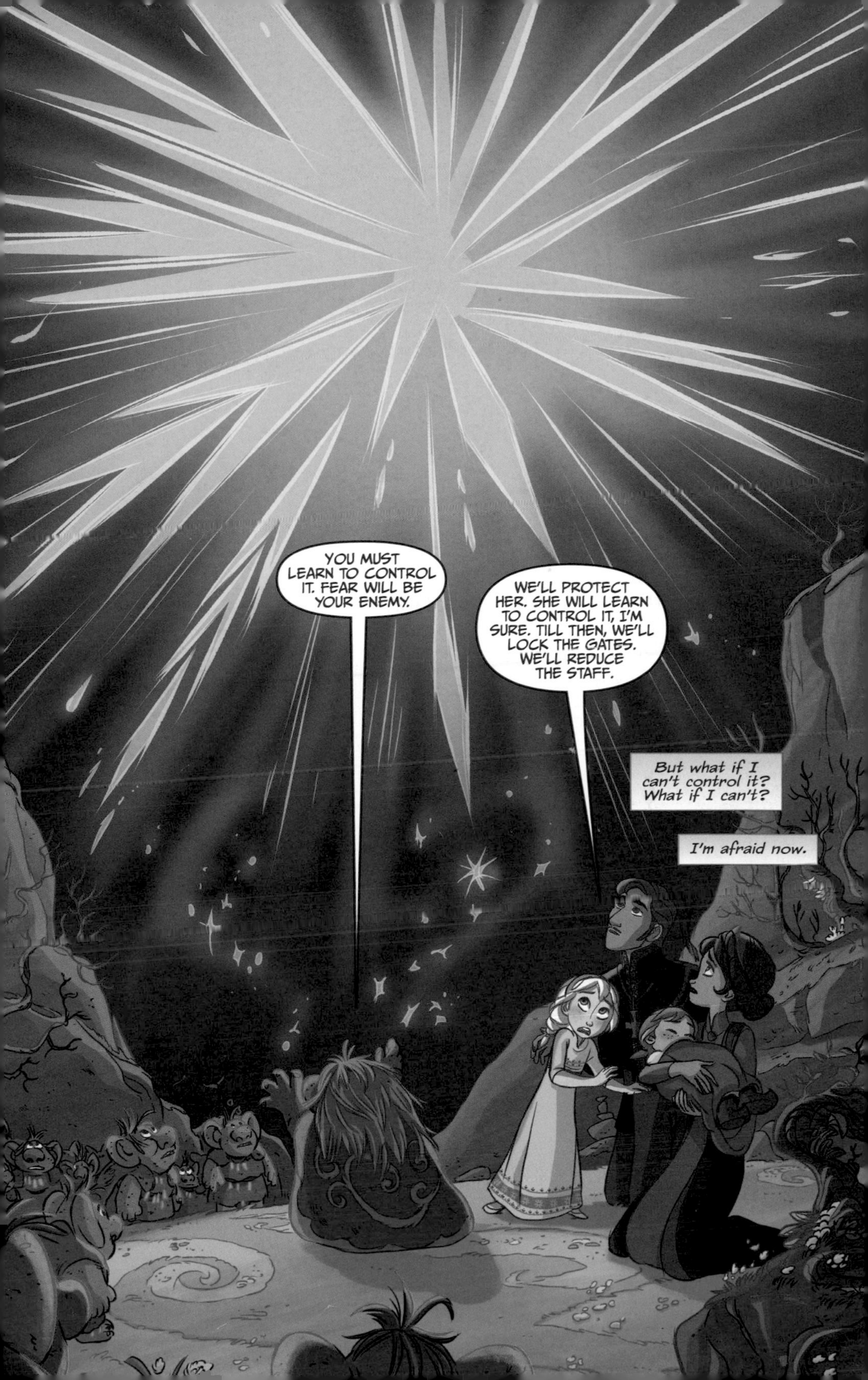
YOU MUST LEARN TO CONTROL IT. FEAR WILL BE YOUR ENEMY.
WE'LL PROTECT HER. SHE WILL LEARN TO CONTROL IT, I'M SURE. TILL THEN, WE'LL LOCK THE GATES. WE'LL REDUCE THE STAFF.
But what if I can't control it? What if I can't?
I'm afraid now.

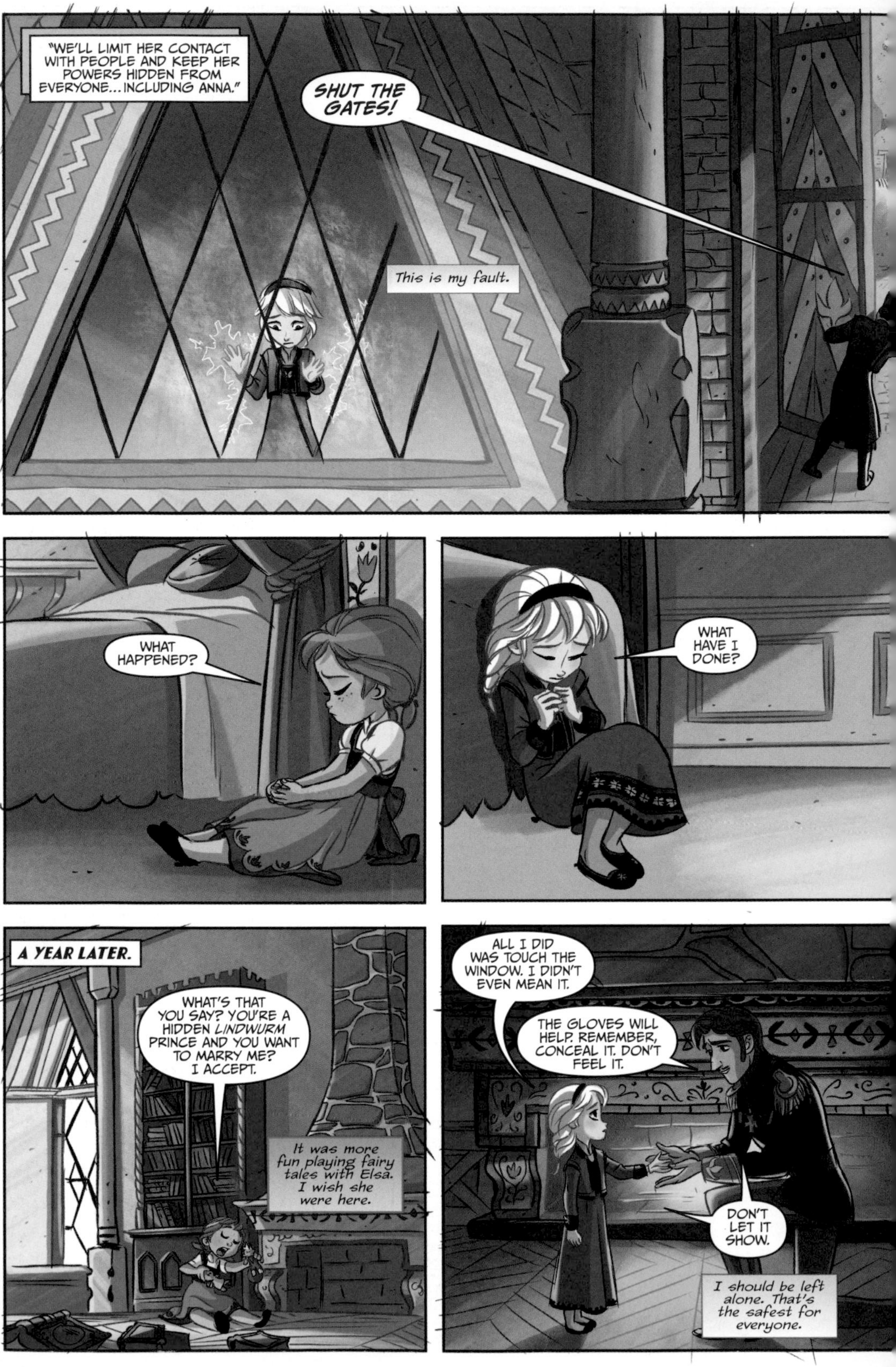
"WE'LL LIMIT HER CONTACT WITH PEOPLE AND KEEP HER POWERS HIDDEN FROM EVERYONE... INCLUDING ANNA."
SHUT THE GATES!
This is my fault.
WHAT HAPPENED?
WHAT HAVE I DONE?
A YEAR LATER.
WHAT'S THAT YOU SAY? YOU'RE A HIDDEN LINDWURM PRINCE AND YOU WANT TO MARRY ME? I ACCEPT.
It was more fun playing fairy tales with Elsa. I wish she were here.
ALL I DID WAS TOUCH THE WINDOW. I DIDN'T EVEN MEAN IT.
THE GLOVES WILL HELP. REMEMBER, CONCEAL IT. DON'T FEEL IT.
DON'T LET IT SHOW.
I should be left alone. That's the safest for everyone.

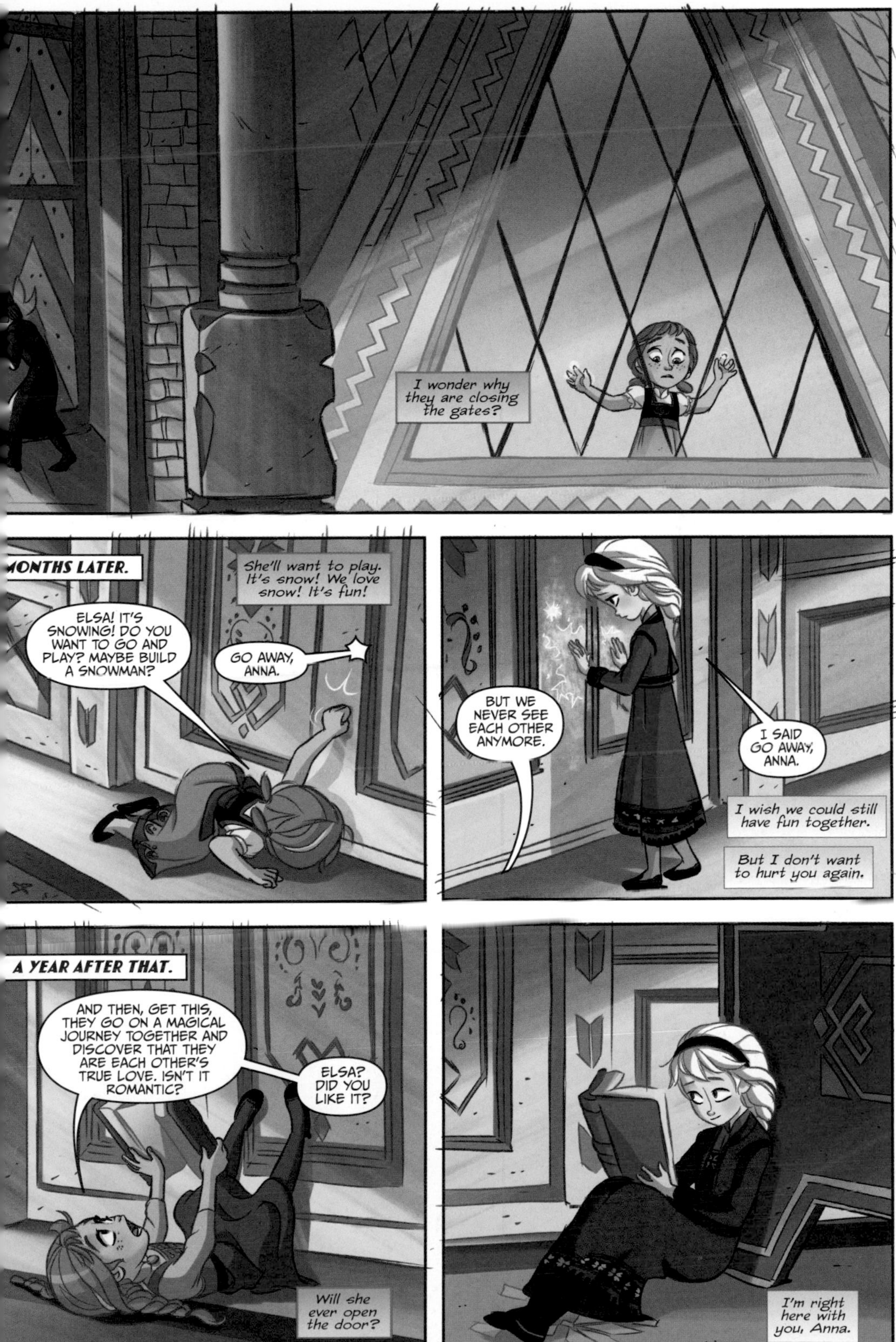

I wonder why they are closing the gates?
MONTHS LATER.
She'll want to play. It's snow! We love snow! It's fun!
ELSA! IT'S SNOWING! DO YOU WANT TO GO AND PLAY? MAYBE BUILD A SNOWMAN?
GO AWAY, ANNA.
BUT WE NEVER SEE EACH OTHER ANYMORE.
I SAID GO AWAY, ANNA.
I wish we could still have fun together.
But I don't want to hurt you again.
A YEAR AFTER THAT.
AND THEN, GET THIS, THEY GO ON A MAGICAL JOURNEY TOGETHER AND DISCOVER THAT THEY ARE EACH OTHER'S TRUE LOVE. ISN'T IT ROMANTIC?
ELSA? DID YOU LIKE IT?
Will she ever open the door?
I'm right here with you, Anna.

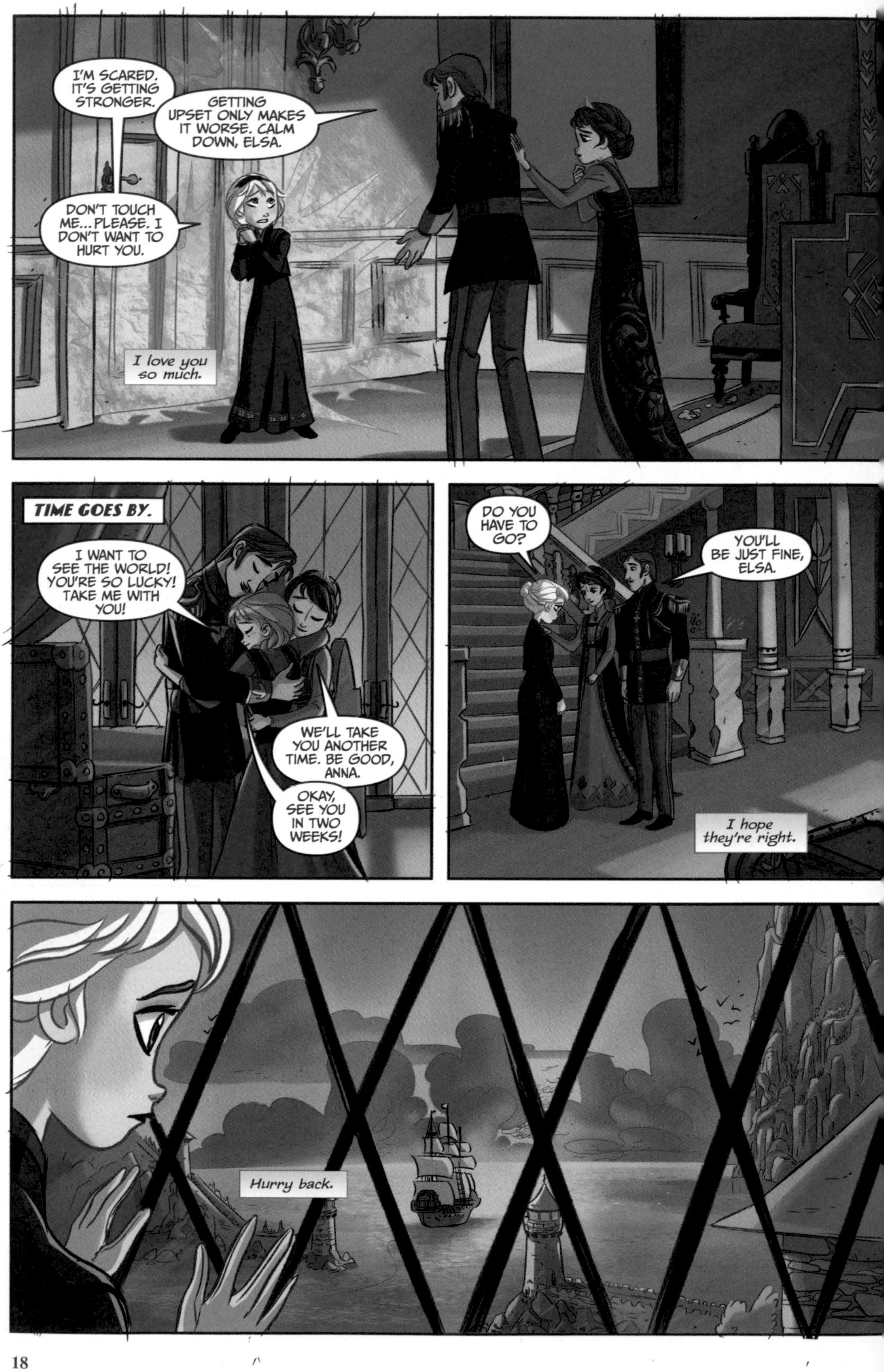
I'M SCARED. IT'S GETTING STRONGER.
GETTING UPSET ONLY MAKES IT WORSE. CALM DOWN, ELSA.
DON'T TOUCH ME...PLEASE. I DON'T WANT TO HURT YOU.
I love you so much.
TIME GOES BY.
I WANT TO SEE THE WORLD! YOU'RE SO LUCKY! TAKE ME WITH YOU!
WE'LL TAKE YOU ANOTHER TIME. BE GOOD, ANNA.
OKAY, SEE YOU IN TWO WEEKS!
DO YOU HAVE TO GO?
YOU'LL BE JUST FINE, ELSA.
I hope they're right.
Hurry back.

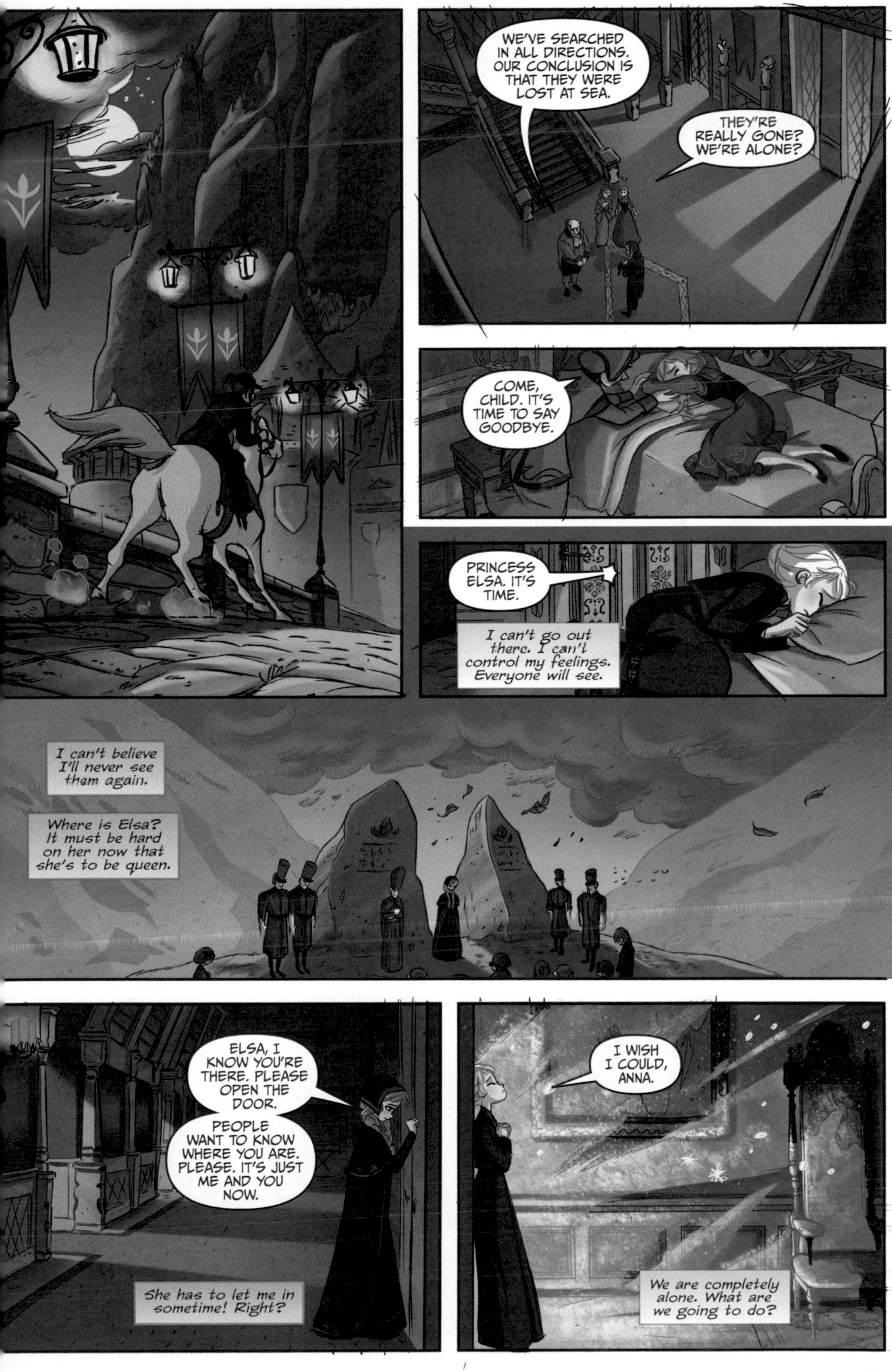
WE'VE SEARCHED IN ALL DIRECTIONS. OUR CONCLUSION IS THAT THEY WERE LOST AT SEA.
THEY'RE REALLY GONE? WE'RE ALONE?
COME, CHILD. IT'S TIME TO SAY GOODBYE.
PRINCESS ELSA. IT'S TIME.
I can't go out there. I can't control my feelings. Everyone will see.
I can't believe I'll never see them again.
Where is Elsa? It must be hard on her now that she's to be queen.
ELSA, I KNOW YOU'RE THERE. PLEASE OPEN THE DOOR.
PEOPLE WANT TO KNOW WHERE YOU ARE. PLEASE. IT'S JUST ME AND YOU NOW.
She has to let me in sometime! Right?
I WISH I COULD, ANNA.
We are completely alone. What are we going to do?

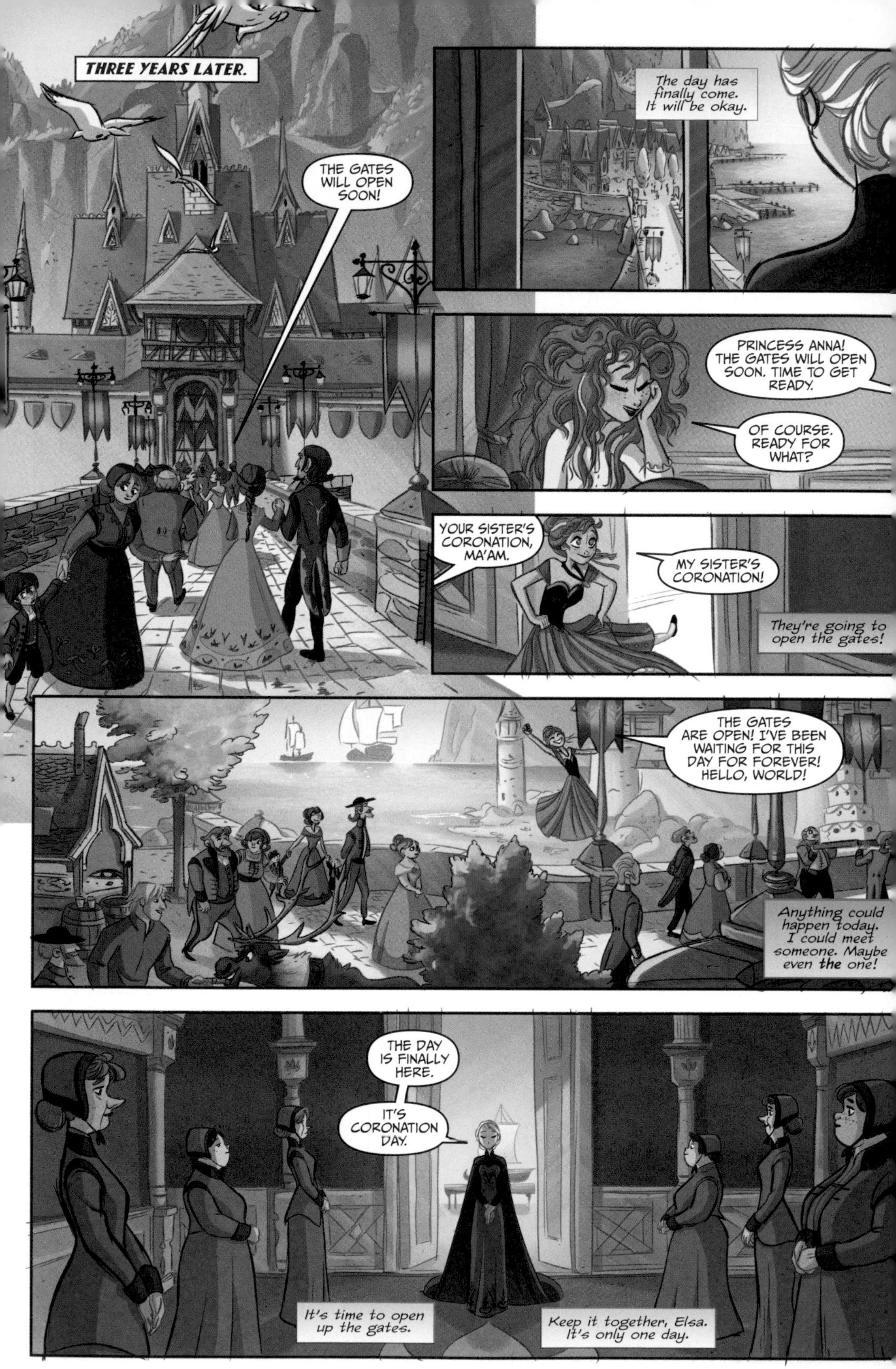
THREE YEARS LATER.
THE GATES WILL OPEN SOON!
The day has finally come. It will be okay.
PRINCESS ANNA! THE GATES WILL OPEN SOON. TIME TO GET READY.
OF COURSE. READY FOR WHAT?
YOUR SISTER'S CORONATION, MA'AM.
MY SISTER'S CORONATION!
They're going to open the gates!
THE GATES ARE OPEN! I'VE BEEN WAITING FOR THIS DAY FOR FOREVER! HELLO, WORLD!
Anything could happen today. I could meet someone. Maybe even the one!
THE DAY IS FINALLY HERE.
IT'S CORONATION DAY.
It's time to open up the gates.
Keep it together, Elsa. It's only one day.

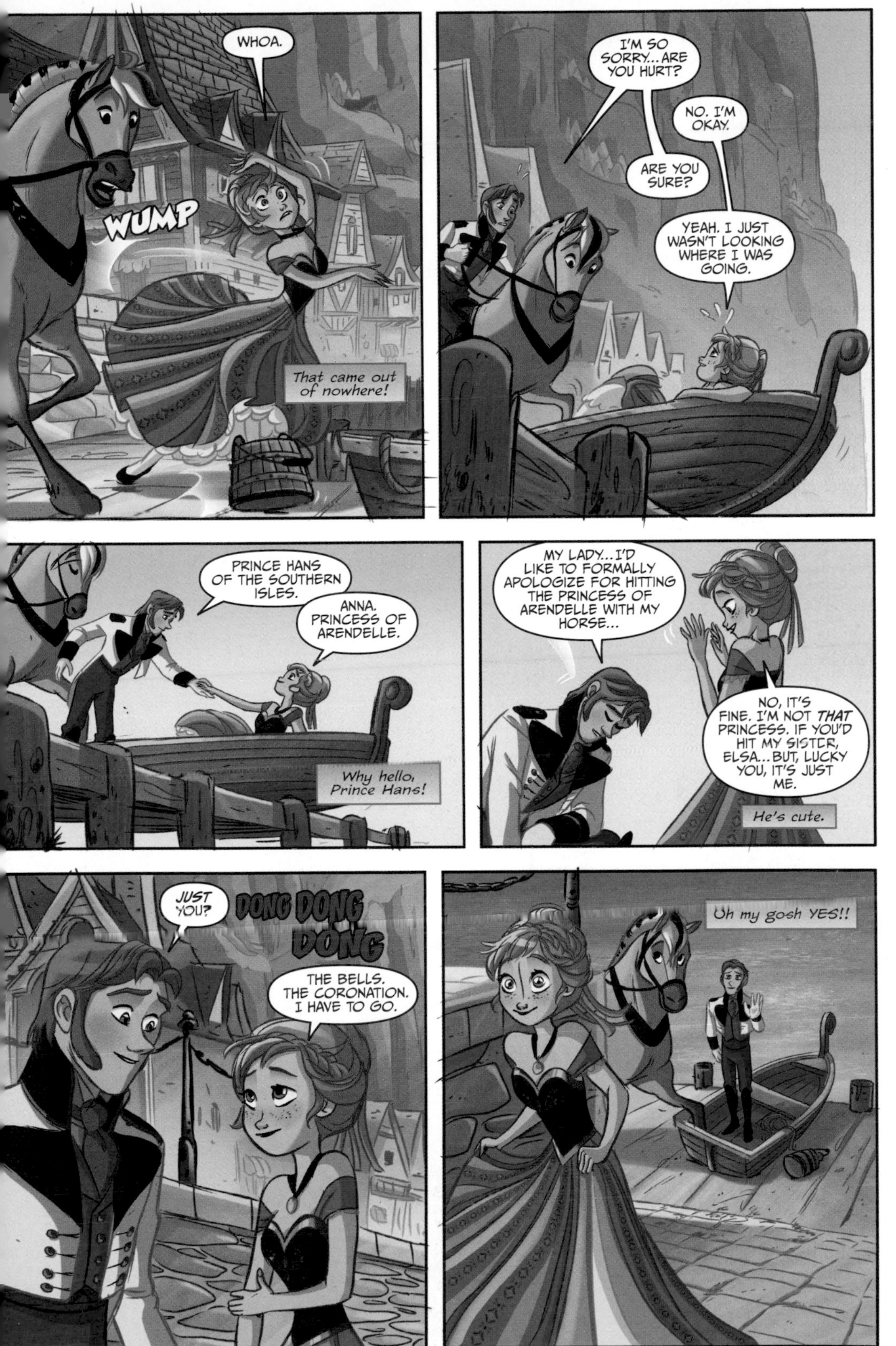
WHOA.
WUMP
That came out of nowhere!
I'M SO SORRY... ARE YOU HURT?
NO. I'M OKAY.
ARE YOU SURE?
YEAH. I JUST WASN'T LOOKING WHERE I WAS GOING.
PRINCE HANS OF THE SOUTHERN ISLES.
ANNA. PRINCESS OF ARENDELLE.
Why hello, Prince Hans!
MY LADY... I'D LIKE TO FORMALLY APOLOGIZE FOR HITTING THE PRINCESS OF ARENDELLE WITH MY HORSE...
NO, IT'S FINE. I'M NOT *THAT* PRINCESS. IF YOU'D HIT MY SISTER, ELSA... BUT, LUCKY YOU, IT'S JUST ME.
He's cute.
JUST YOU?
DONG DONG DONG
THE BELLS. THE CORONATION. I HAVE TO GO.
Uh my gosh YES!!

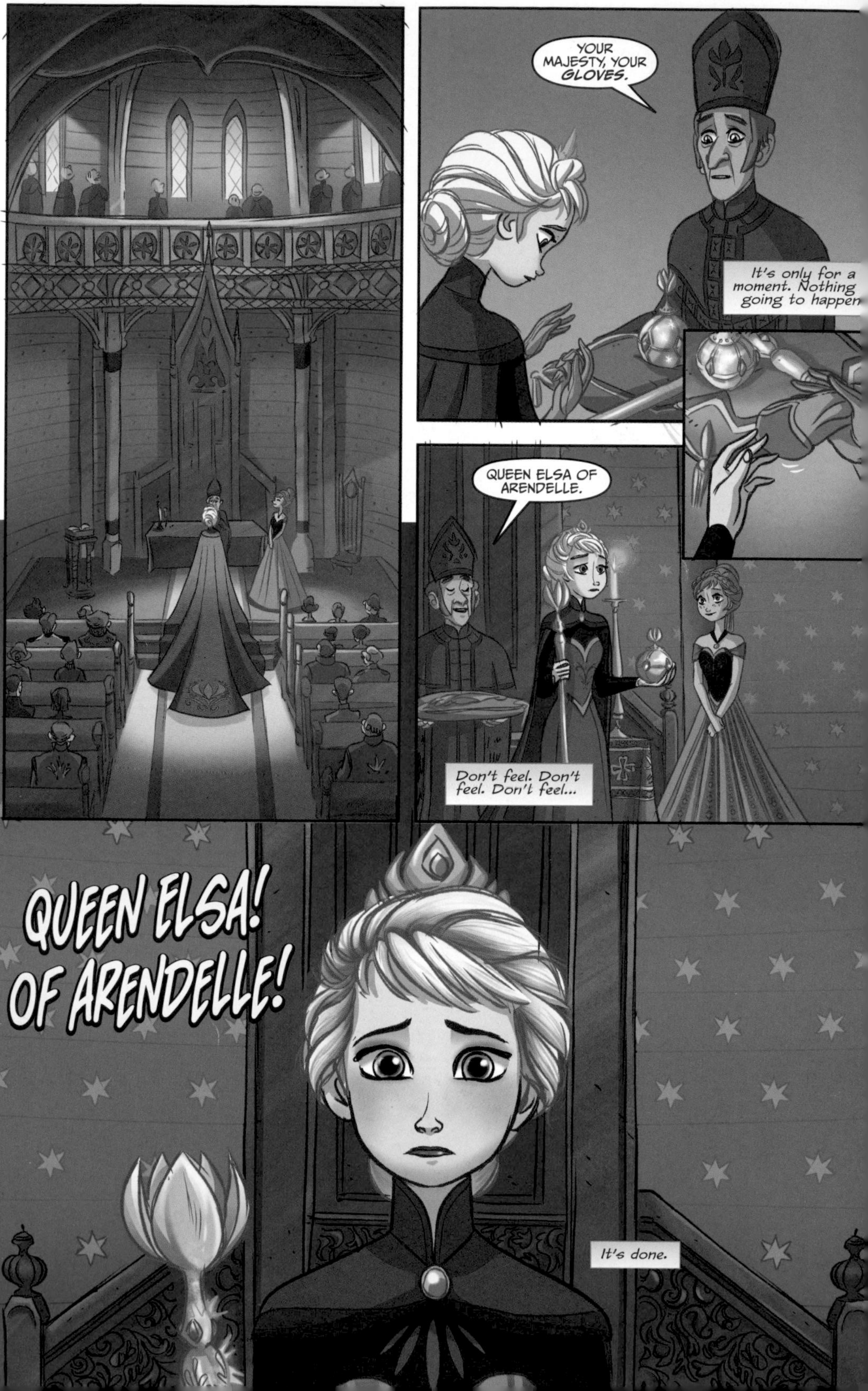
YOUR MAJESTY, YOUR GLOVES.
It's only for a moment. Nothing going to happen
QUEEN ELSA OF ARENDELLE.
Don't feel. Don't feel. Don't feel...
QUEEN ELSA! OF ARENDELLE!
It's done.

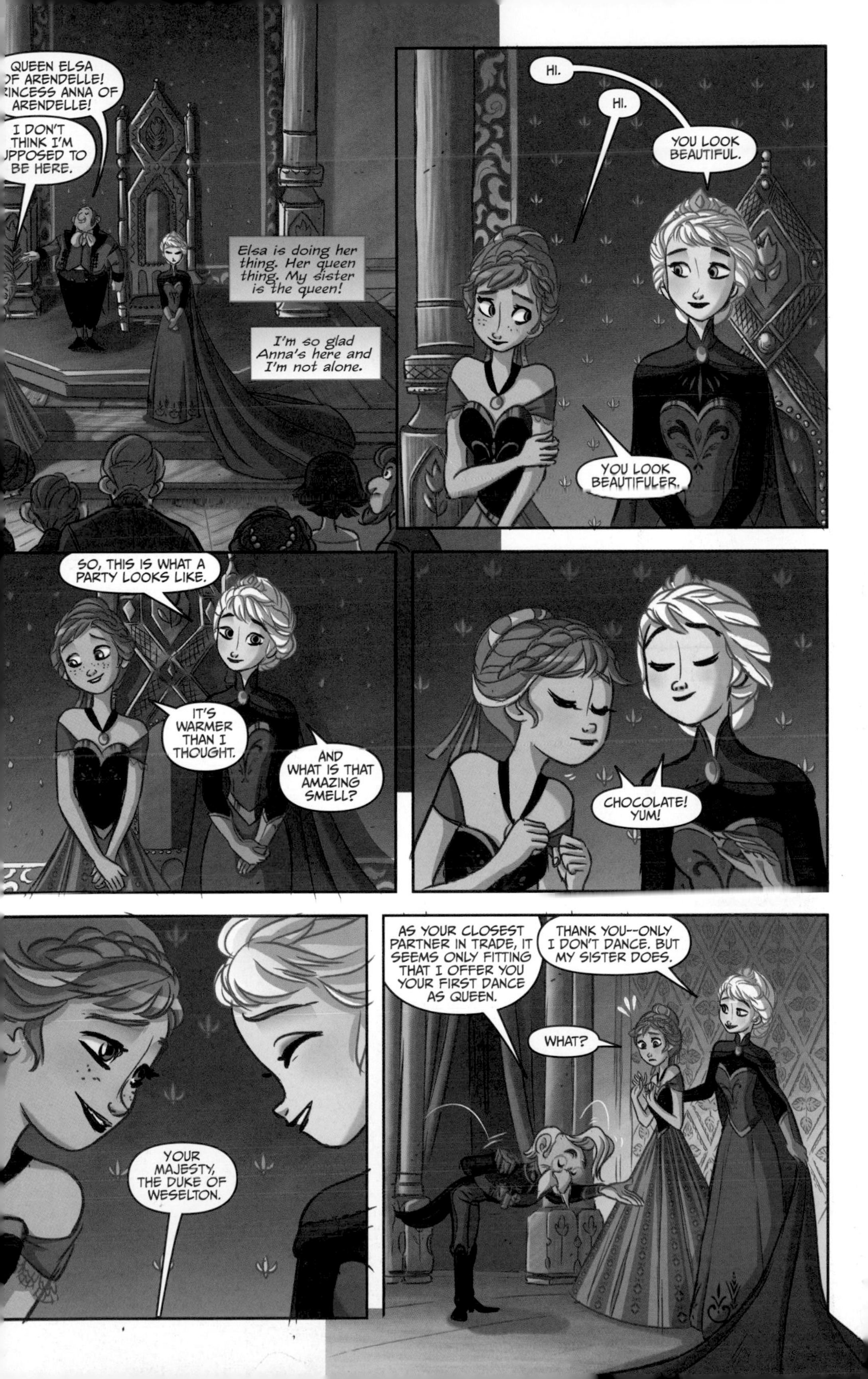
QUEEN ELSA OF ARENDELLE! PRINCESS ANNA OF ARENDELLE!
I DON'T THINK I'M SUPPOSED TO BE HERE.
Elsa is doing her thing. Her queen thing. My sister is the queen!
I'm so glad Anna's here and I'm not alone.
HI.
HI.
YOU LOOK BEAUTIFUL.
YOU LOOK BEAUTIFULER.
SO, THIS IS WHAT A PARTY LOOKS LIKE.
IT'S WARMER THAN I THOUGHT.
AND WHAT IS THAT AMAZING SMELL?
CHOCOLATE! YUM!
YOUR MAJESTY, THE DUKE OF WESELTON.
AS YOUR CLOSEST PARTNER IN TRADE, IT SEEMS ONLY FITTING THAT I OFFER YOU YOUR FIRST DANCE AS QUEEN.
THANK YOU--ONLY I DON'T DANCE. BUT MY SISTER DOES.
WHAT?

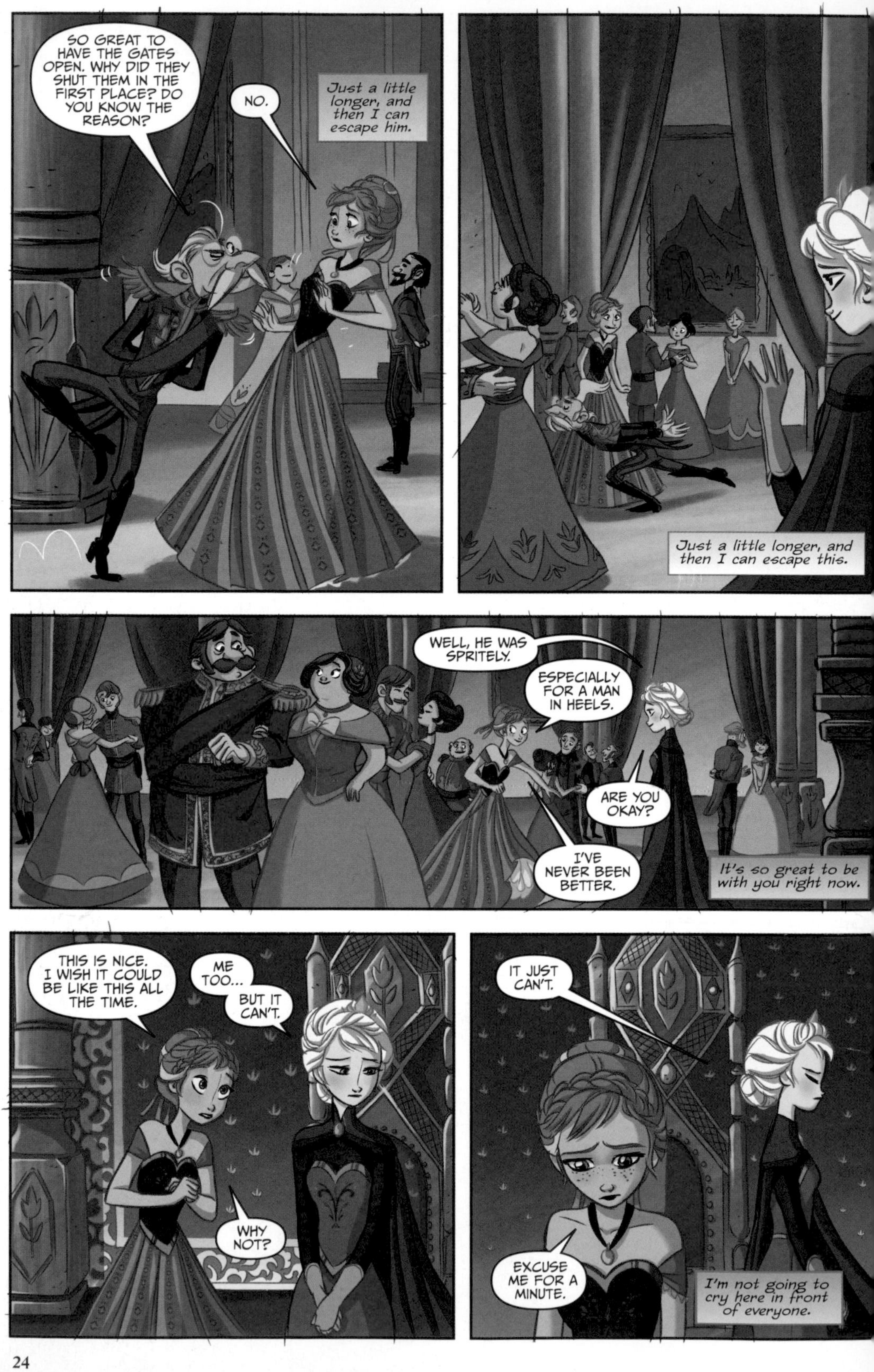
SO GREAT TO HAVE THE GATES OPEN. WHY DID THEY SHUT THEM IN THE FIRST PLACE? DO YOU KNOW THE REASON?
NO.
Just a little longer, and then I can escape him.
Just a little longer, and then I can escape this.
WELL, HE WAS SPRITELY.
ESPECIALLY FOR A MAN IN HEELS.
ARE YOU OKAY?
I'VE NEVER BEEN BETTER.
It's so great to be with you right now.
THIS IS NICE. I WISH IT COULD BE LIKE THIS ALL THE TIME.
ME TOO... BUT IT CAN'T.
WHY NOT?
IT JUST CAN'T.
EXCUSE ME FOR A MINUTE.
I'm not going to cry here in front of everyone.

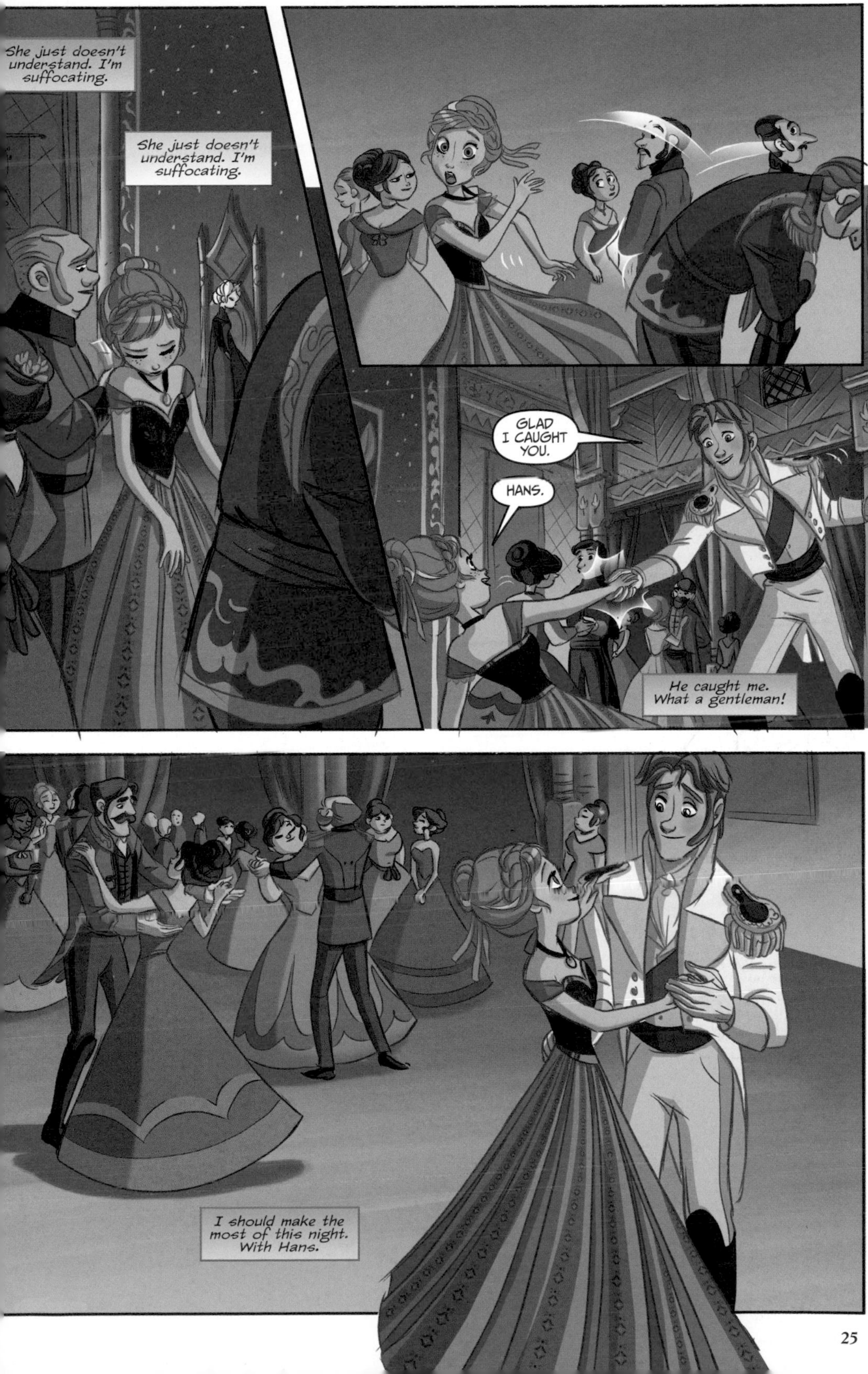
She just doesn't understand. I'm suffocating.
She just doesn't understand. I'm suffocating.
GLAD I CAUGHT YOU.
HANS.
He caught me. What a gentleman!
I should make the most of this night. With Hans.

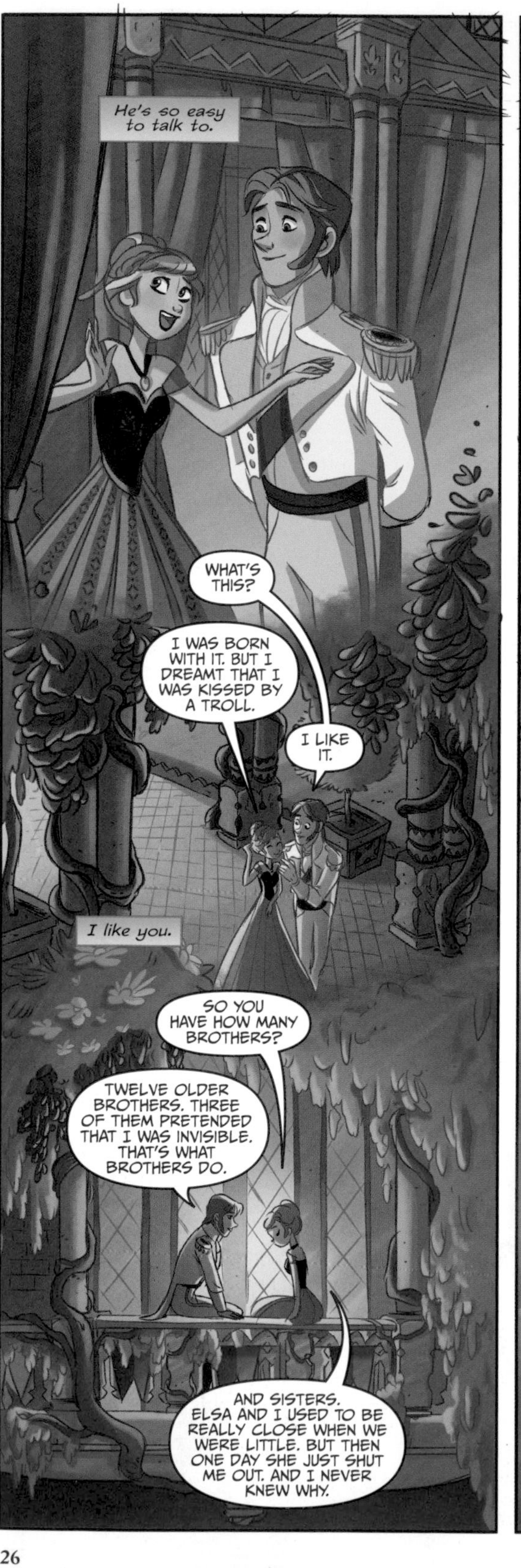
He's so easy to talk to.
WHAT'S THIS?
I WAS BORN WITH IT. BUT I DREAMT THAT I WAS KISSED BY A TROLL.
I LIKE IT.
I like you.
SO YOU HAVE HOW MANY BROTHERS?
TWELVE OLDER BROTHERS. THREE OF THEM PRETENDED THAT I WAS INVISIBLE. THAT'S WHAT BROTHERS DO.
AND SISTERS. ELSA AND I USED TO BE REALLY CLOSE WHEN WE WERE LITTLE. BUT THEN ONE DAY SHE JUST SHUT ME OUT. AND I NEVER KNEW WHY.

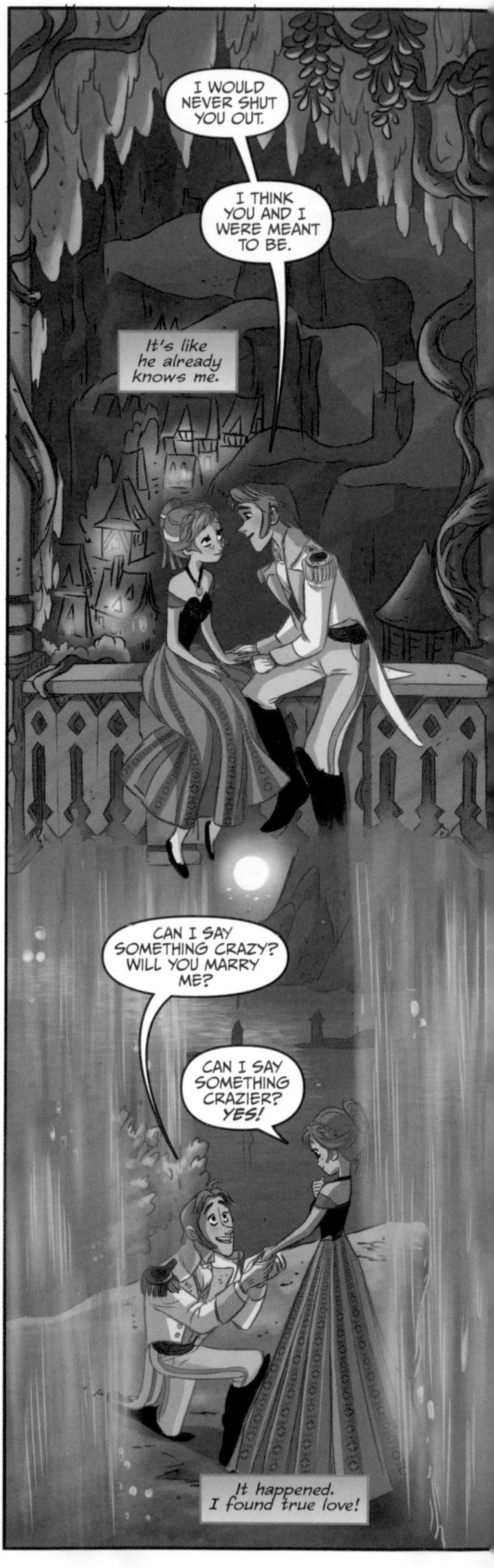
I WOULD NEVER SHUT YOU OUT.
I THINK YOU AND I WERE MEANT TO BE.
It's like he already knows me.
CAN I SAY SOMETHING CRAZY? WILL YOU MARRY ME?
CAN I SAY SOMETHING CRAZIER? YES!
It happened. I found true love!

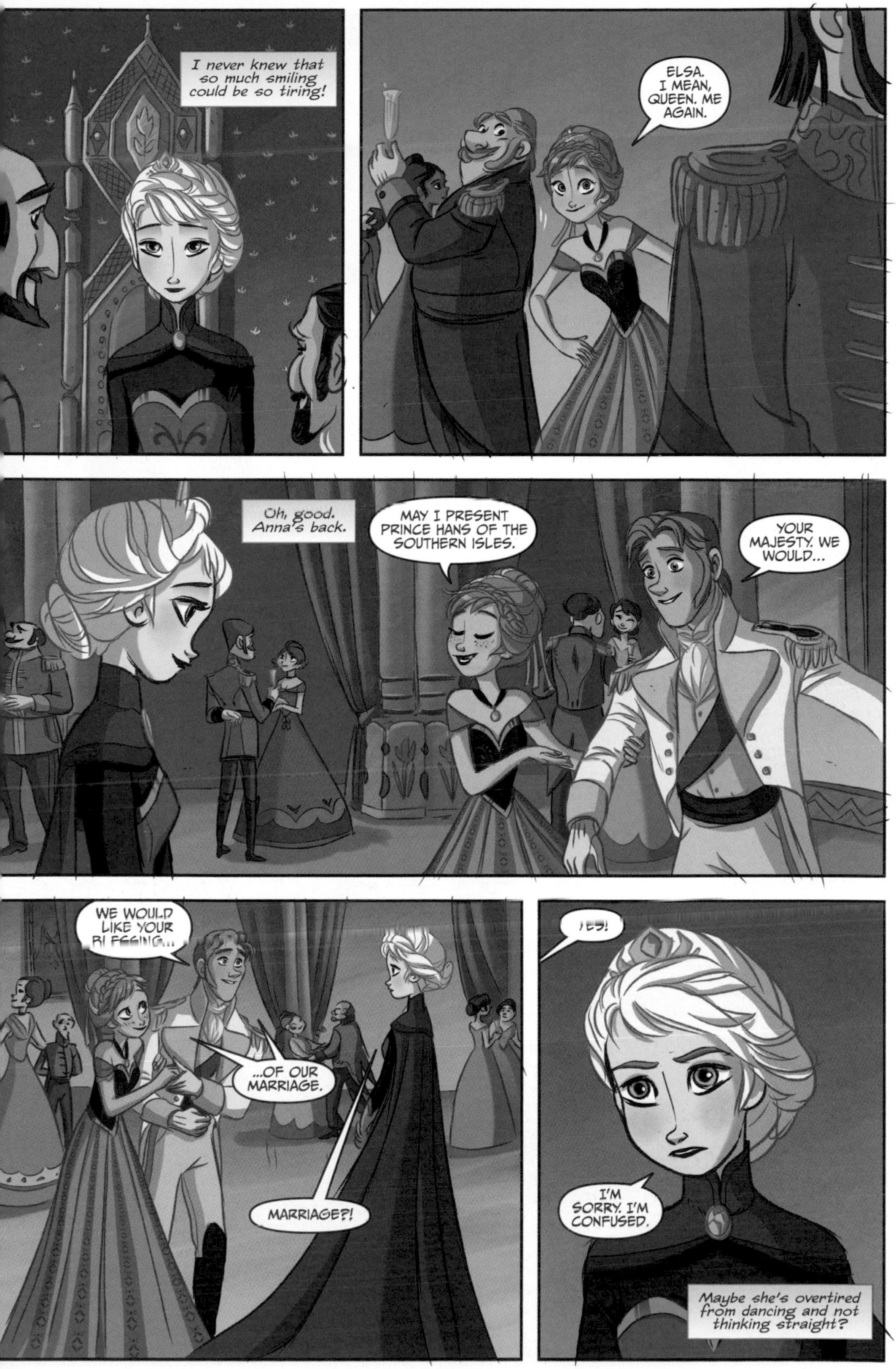
I never knew that so much smiling could be so tiring!
ELSA. I MEAN, QUEEN. ME AGAIN.
Oh, good. Anna's back.
MAY I PRESENT PRINCE HANS OF THE SOUTHERN ISLES.
YOUR MAJESTY. WE WOULD...
WE WOULD LIKE YOUR
...OF OUR MARRIAGE.
MARRIAGE?!
I'M SORRY. I'M CONFUSED.
Maybe she's overtired from dancing and not thinking straight?

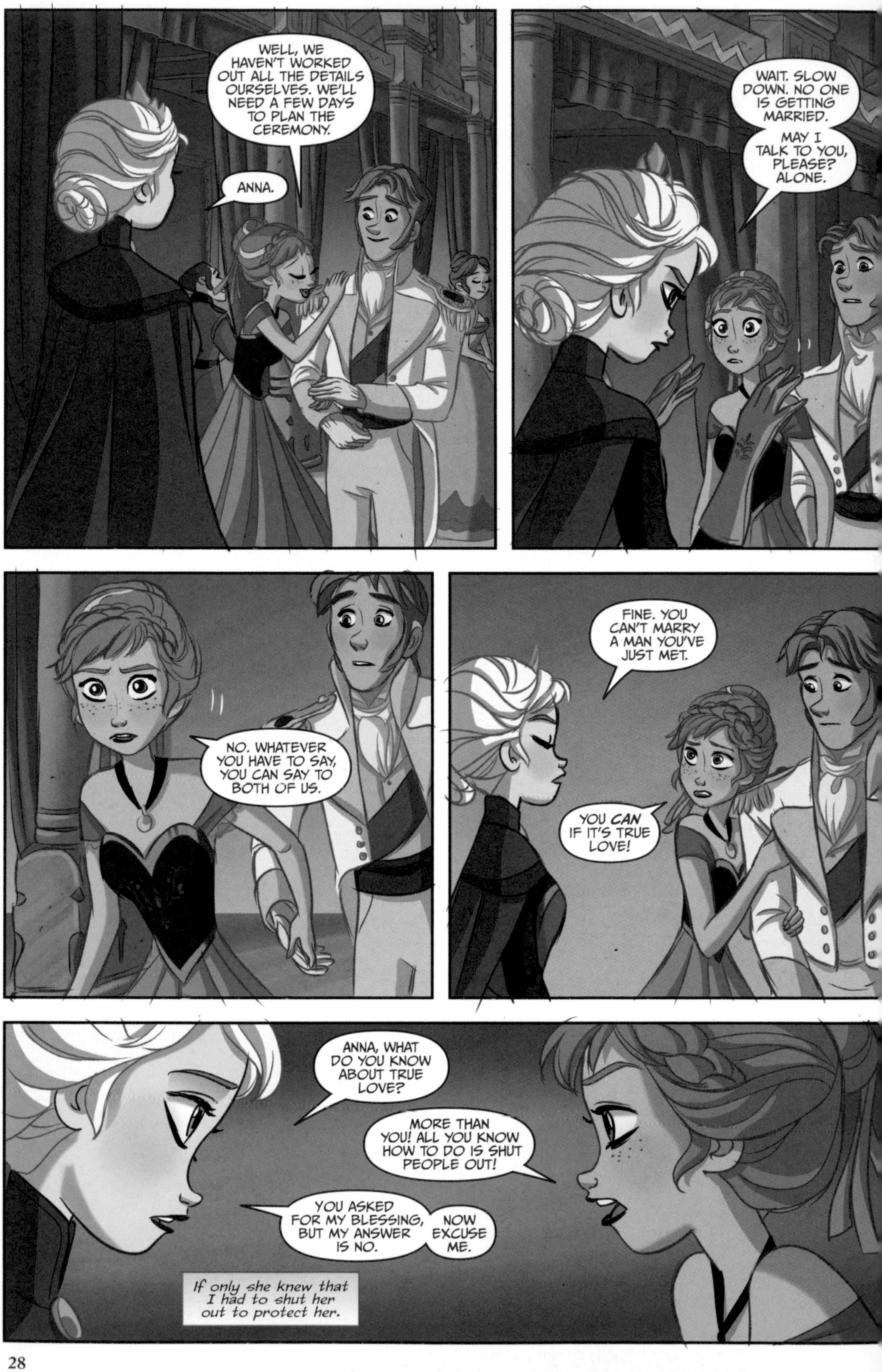
WELL, WE HAVEN'T WORKED OUT ALL THE DETAILS OURSELVES. WE'LL NEED A FEW DAYS TO PLAN THE CEREMONY.
ANNA.
WAIT. SLOW DOWN. NO ONE IS GETTING MARRIED.
MAY I TALK TO YOU, PLEASE? ALONE.
NO. WHATEVER YOU HAVE TO SAY, YOU CAN SAY TO BOTH OF US.
FINE. YOU CAN'T MARRY A MAN YOU'VE JUST MET.
YOU *CAN* IF IT'S TRUE LOVE!
ANNA, WHAT DO YOU KNOW ABOUT TRUE LOVE?
MORE THAN YOU! ALL YOU KNOW HOW TO DO IS SHUT PEOPLE OUT!
YOU ASKED FOR MY BLESSING, BUT MY ANSWER IS NO.
NOW EXCUSE ME.
If only she knew that I had to shut her out to protect her.

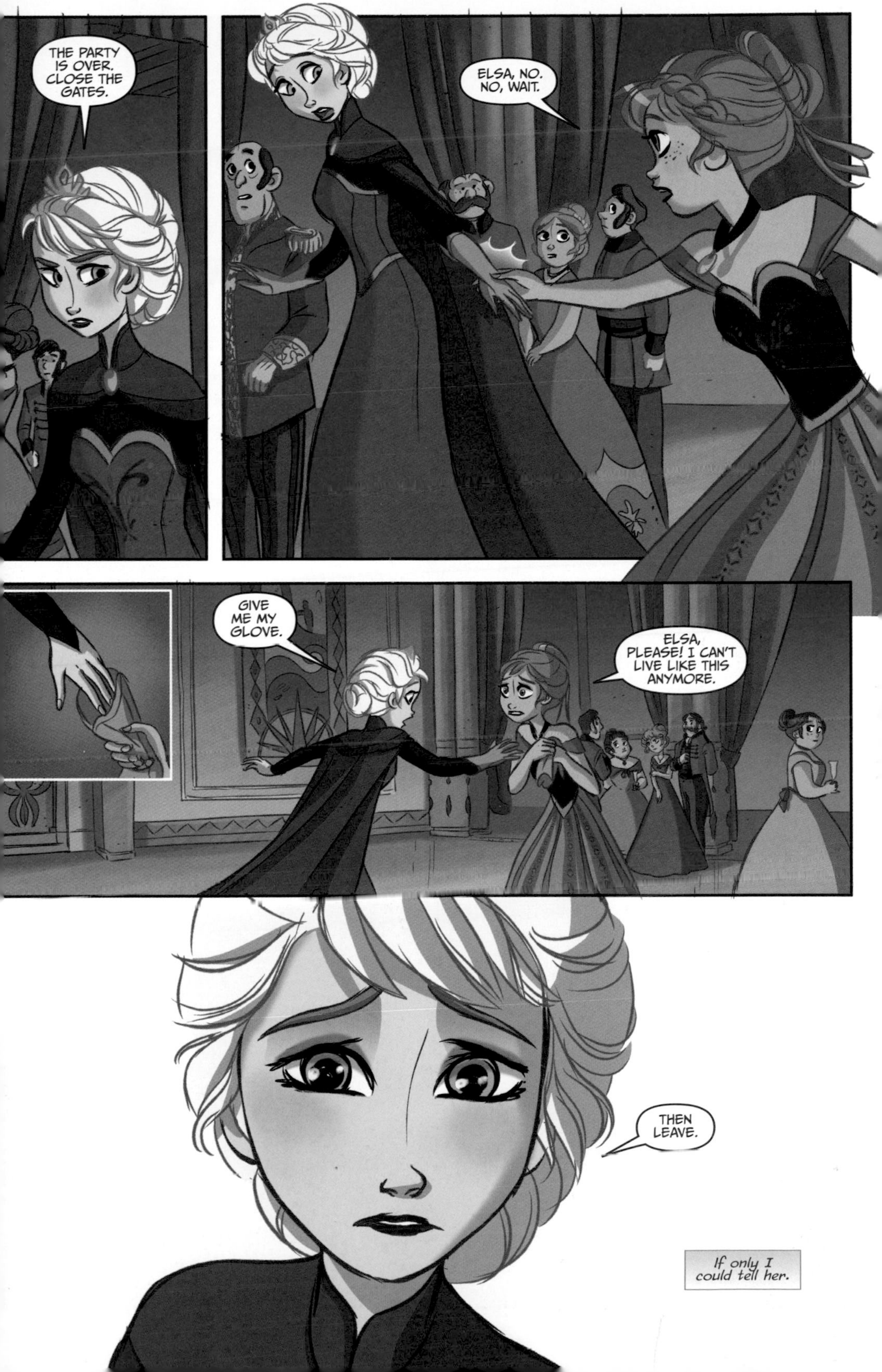
THE PARTY IS OVER. CLOSE THE GATES.
ELSA, NO. NO, WAIT.
GIVE ME MY GLOVE.
ELSA, PLEASE! I CAN'T LIVE LIKE THIS ANYMORE.
THEN LEAVE.
If only I could tell her.

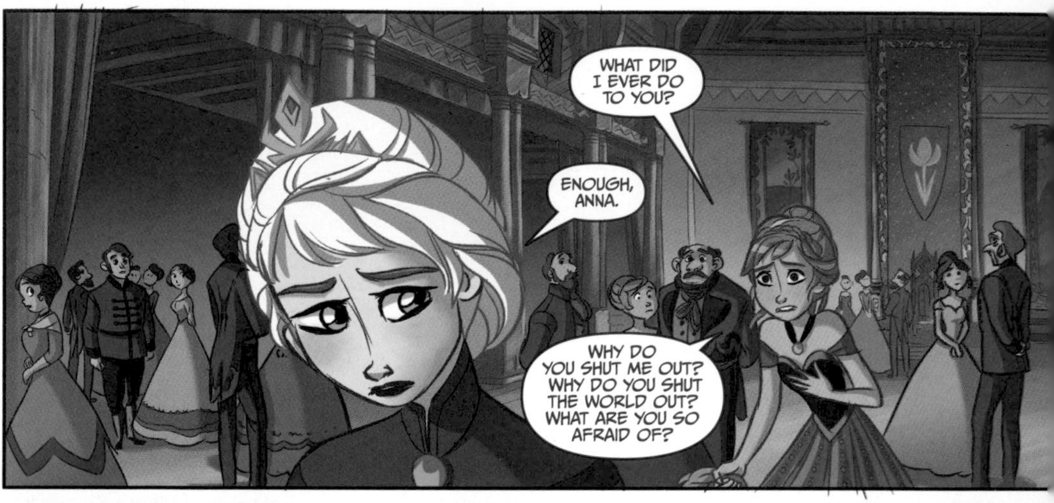
WHAT DID I EVER DO TO YOU?
ENOUGH, ANNA.
WHY DO YOU SHUT ME OUT? WHY DO YOU SHUT THE WORLD OUT? WHAT ARE YOU SO AFRAID OF?

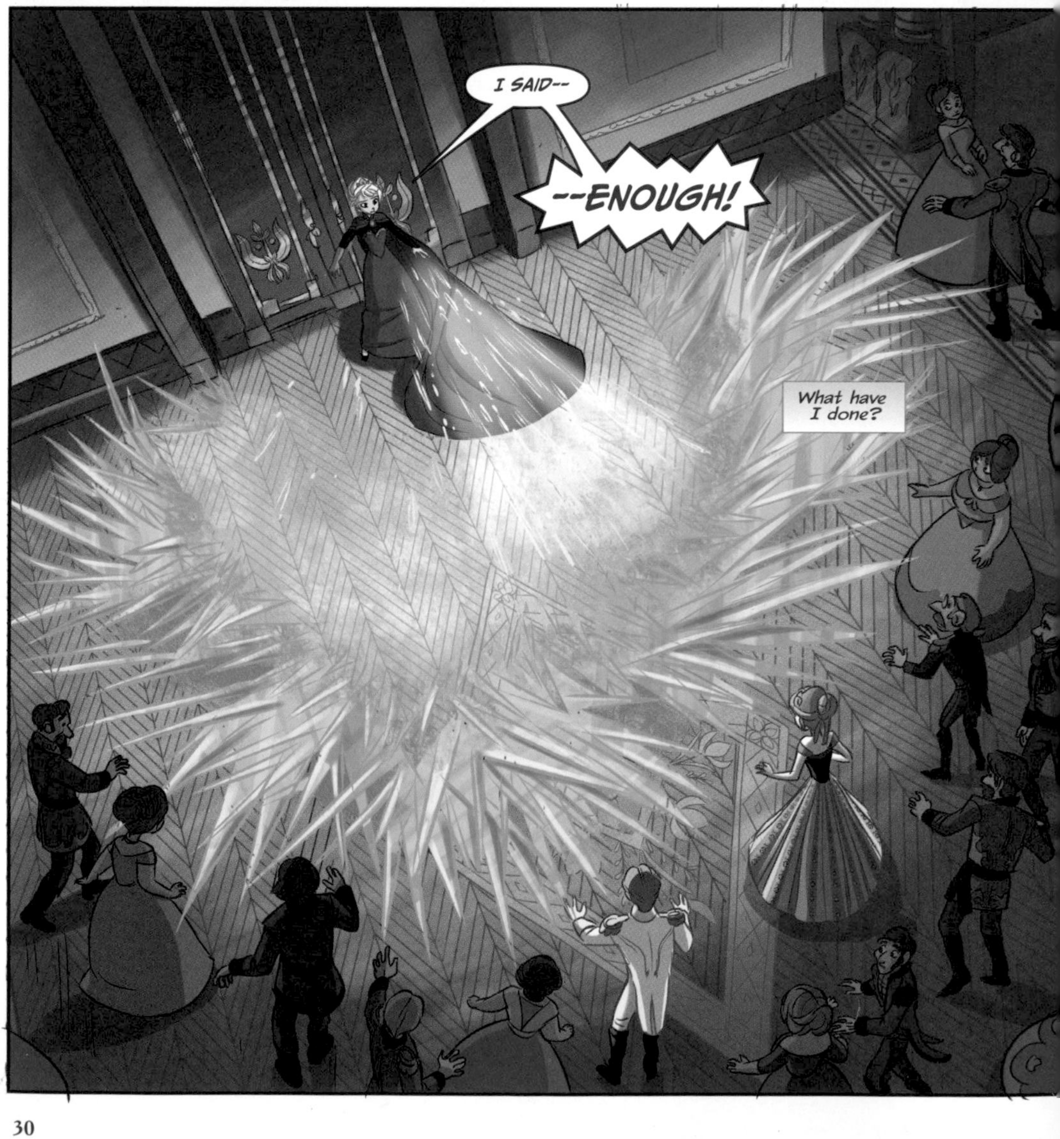
I SAID--
--ENOUGH!
What have I done?

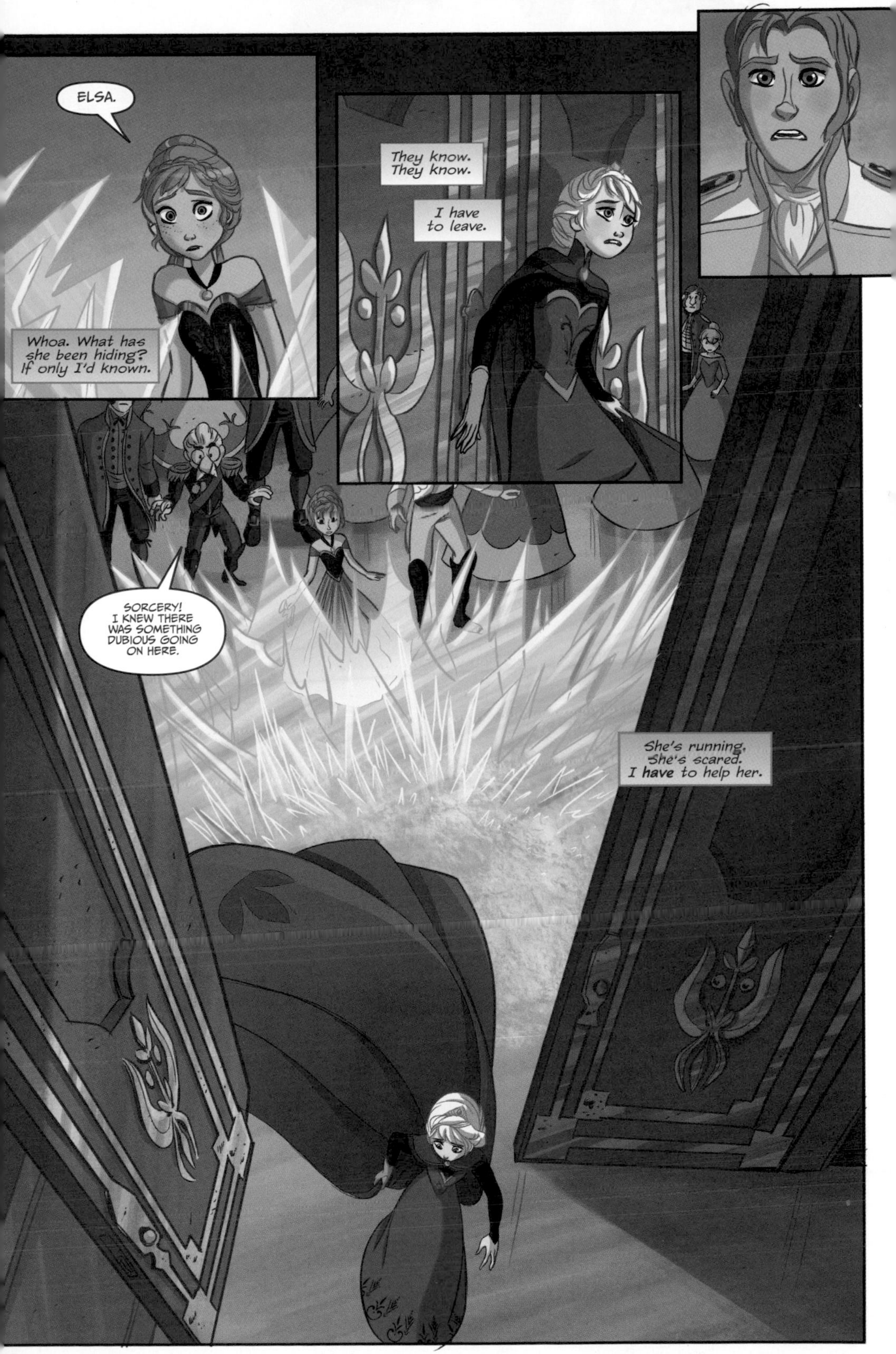
ELSA.
Whoa. What has she been hiding? If only I'd known.
They know. They know.
I have to leave.
SORCERY! I KNEW THERE WAS SOMETHING DUBIOUS GOING ON HERE.
She's running. She's scared. I **have** to help her.

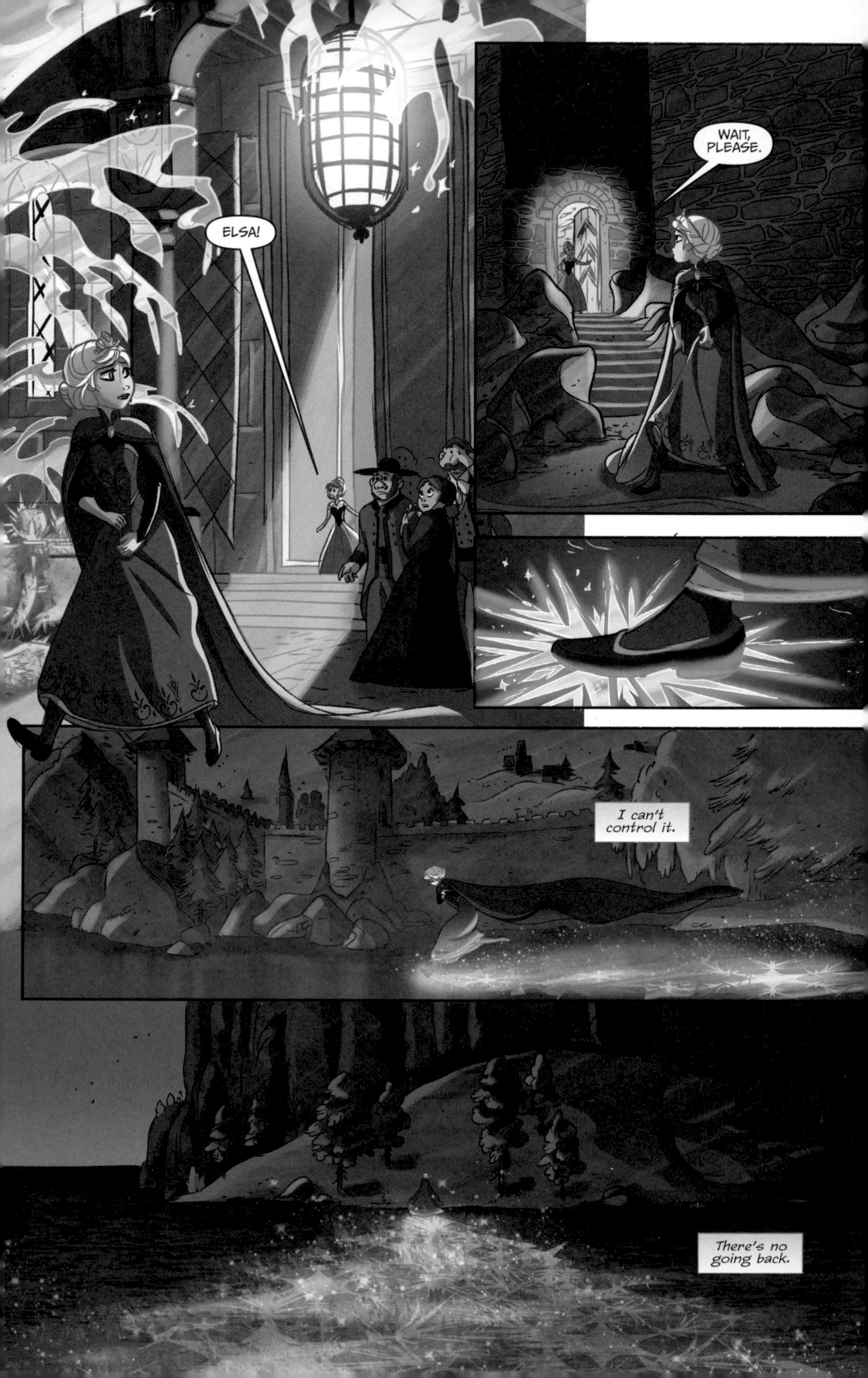
ELSA!
WAIT, PLEASE.
I can't control it.
There's no going back.

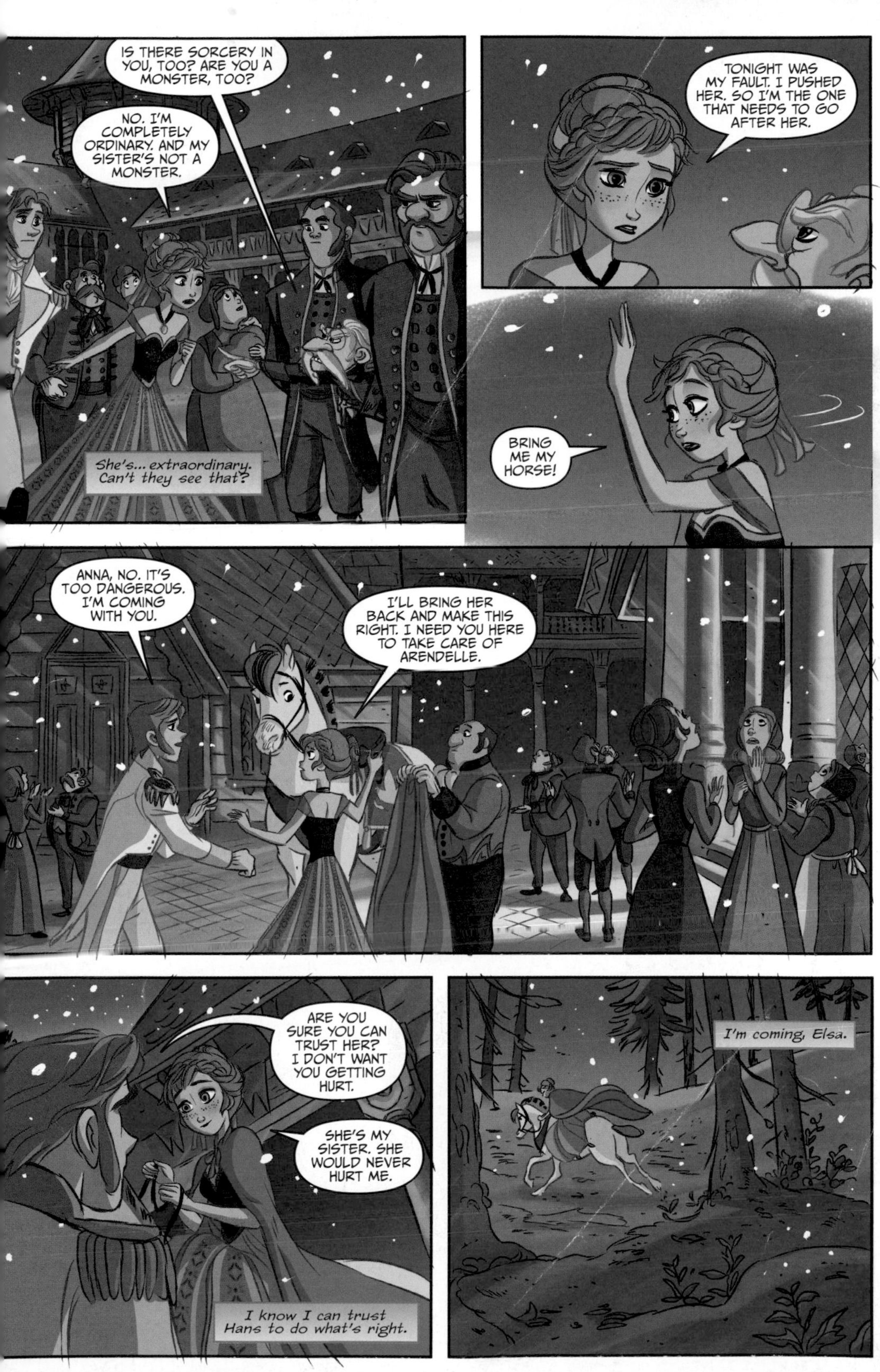
IS THERE SORCERY IN YOU, TOO? ARE YOU A MONSTER, TOO?
NO. I'M COMPLETELY ORDINARY. AND MY SISTER'S NOT A MONSTER.
She's... extraordinary. Can't they see that?
TONIGHT WAS MY FAULT. I PUSHED HER. SO I'M THE ONE THAT NEEDS TO GO AFTER HER.
BRING ME MY HORSE!
ANNA, NO. IT'S TOO DANGEROUS. I'M COMING WITH YOU.
I'LL BRING HER BACK AND MAKE THIS RIGHT. I NEED YOU HERE TO TAKE CARE OF ARENDELLE.
ARE YOU SURE YOU CAN TRUST HER? I DON'T WANT YOU GETTING HURT.
SHE'S MY SISTER. SHE WOULD NEVER HURT ME.
I know I can trust Hans to do what's right.
I'm coming, Elsa.

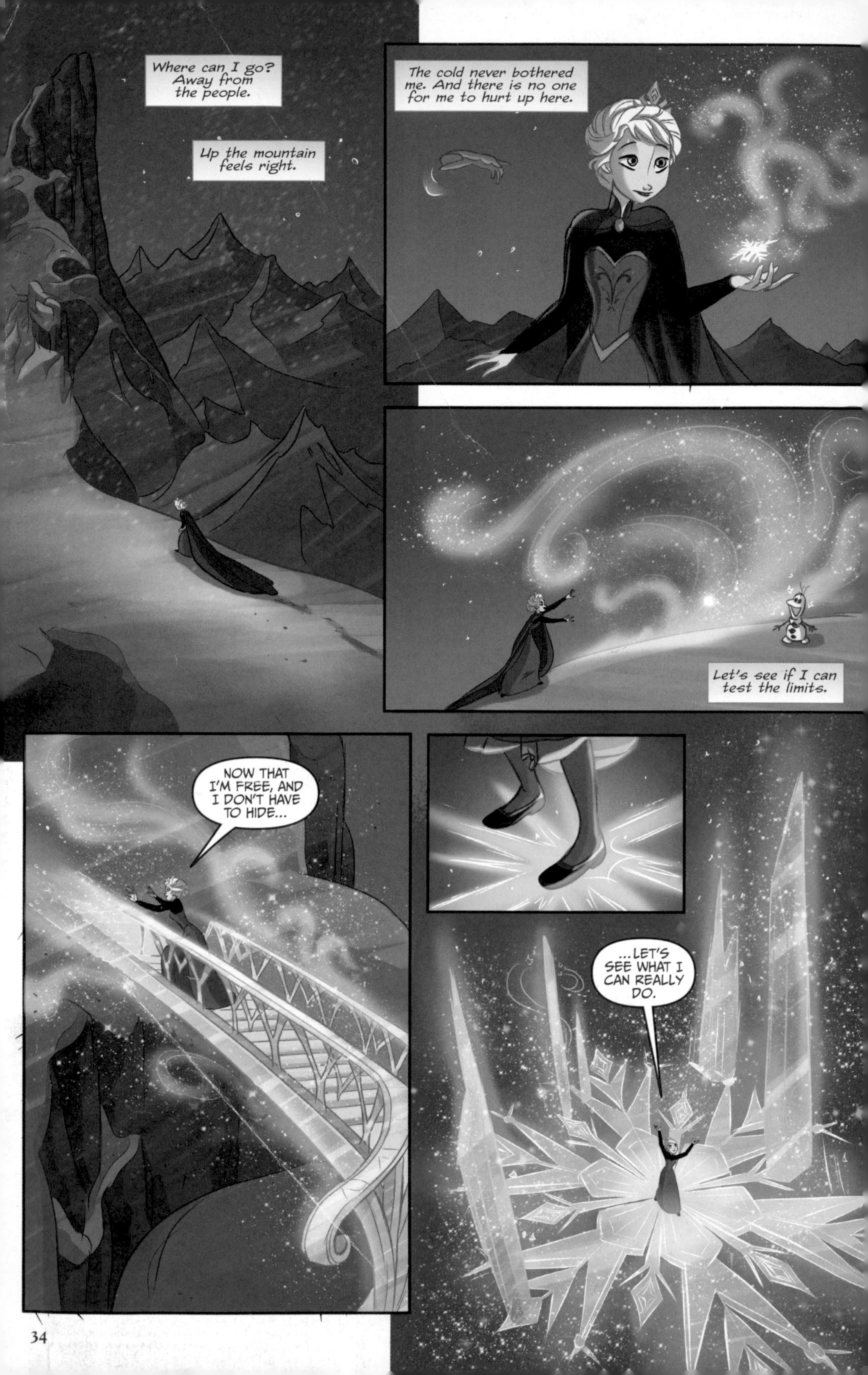

Where can I go? Away from the people.
Up the mountain feels right.
The cold never bothered me. And there is no one for me to hurt up here.
Let's see if I can test the limits.
NOW THAT I'M FREE, AND I DON'T HAVE TO HIDE...
...LET'S SEE WHAT I CAN REALLY DO.

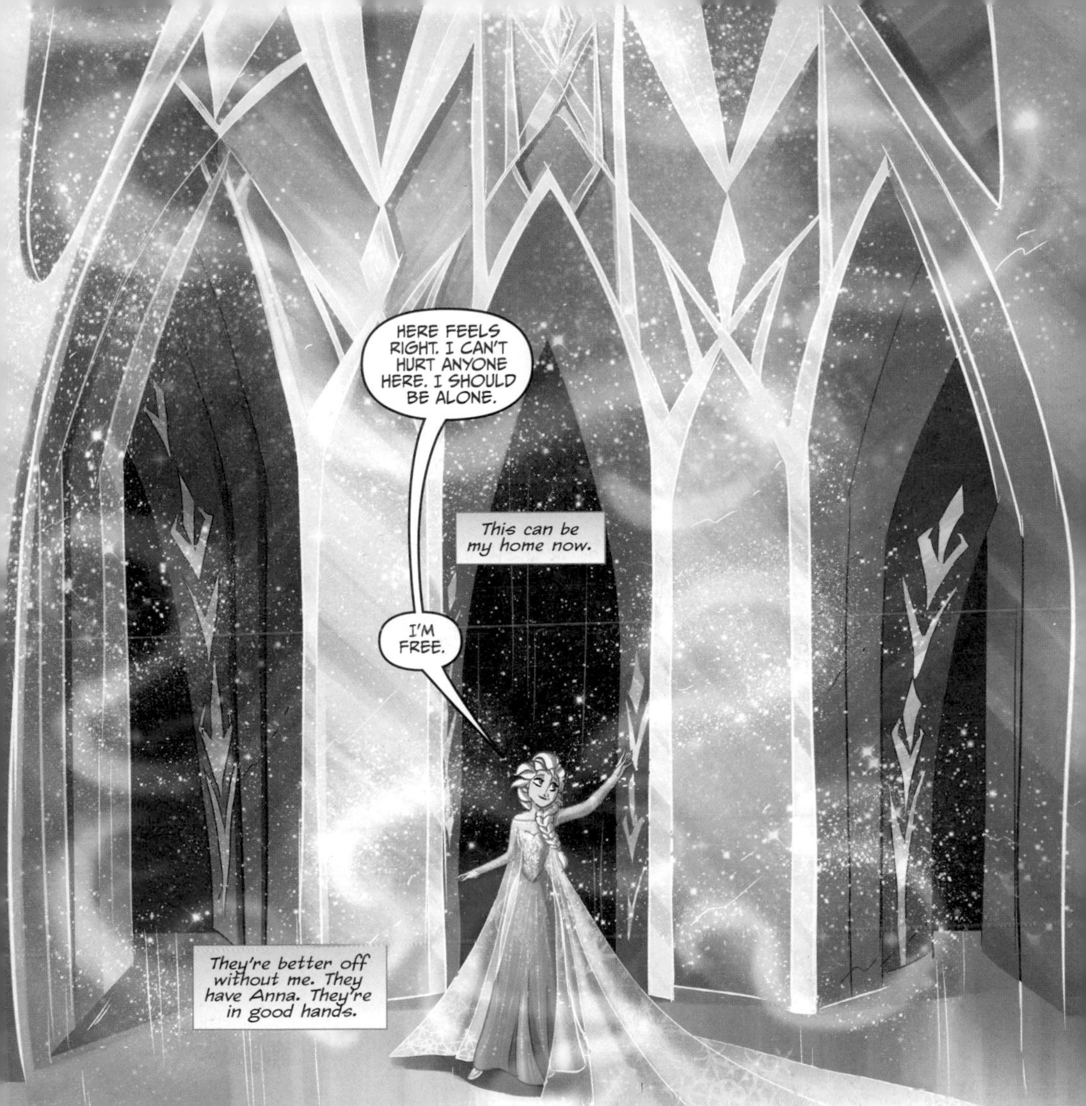
HERE FEELS RIGHT. I CAN'T HURT ANYONE HERE. I SHOULD BE ALONE.
This can be my home now.
I'M FREE.
They're better off without me. They have Anna. They're in good hands.
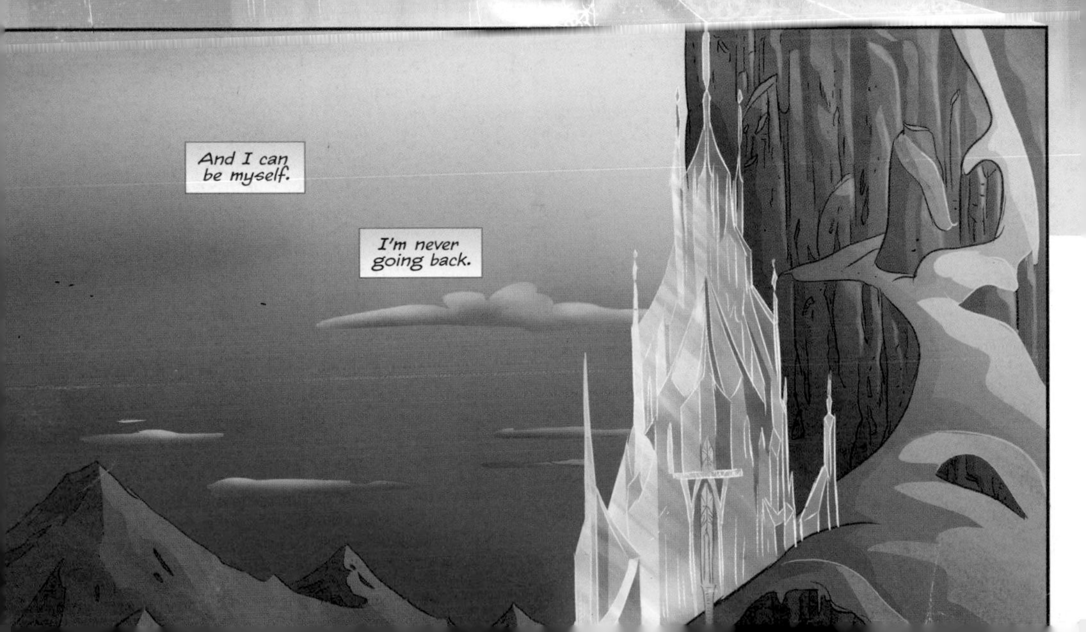
And I can be myself.
I'm never going back.

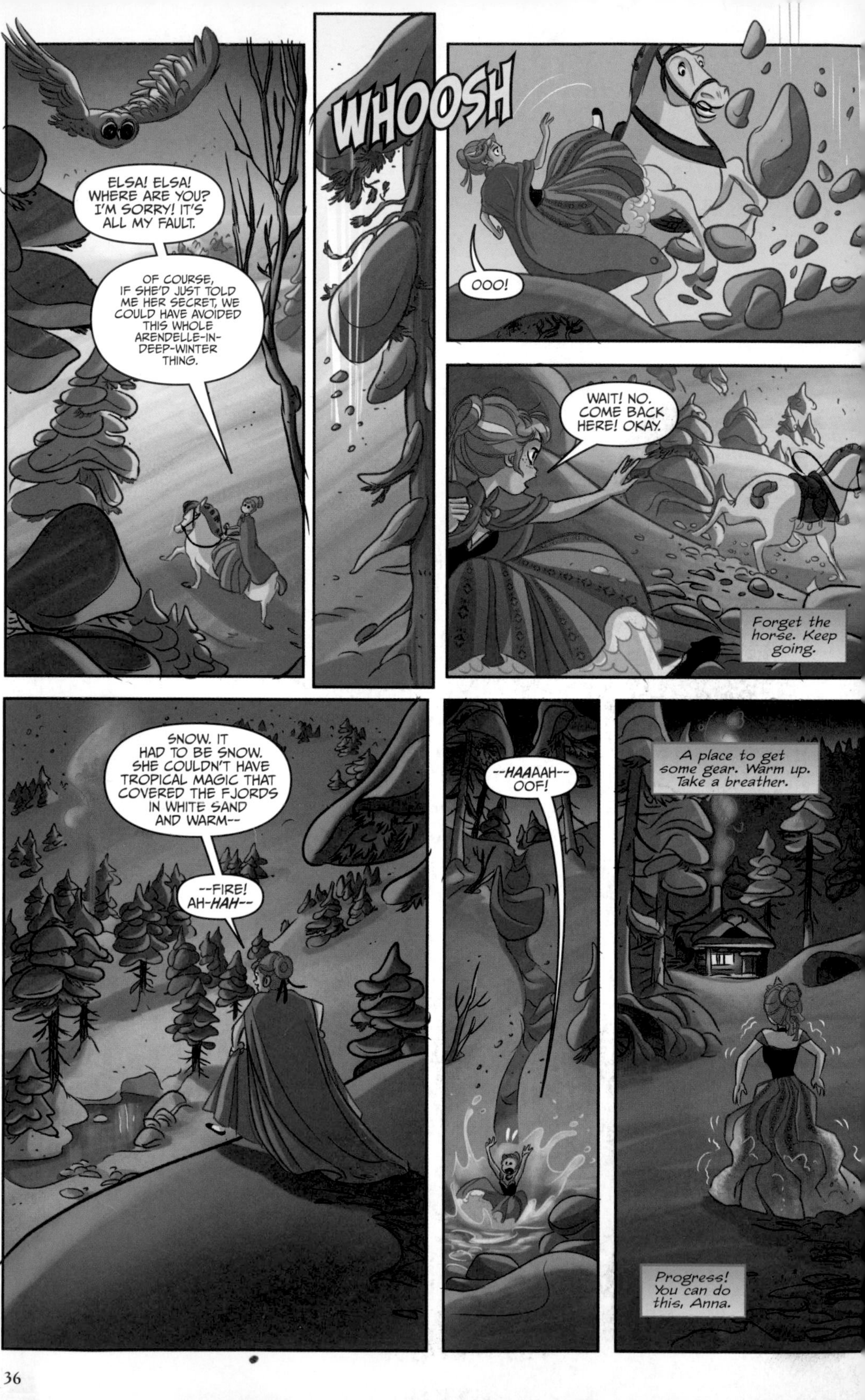

ELSA! ELSA! WHERE ARE YOU? I'M SORRY! IT'S ALL MY FAULT.
OF COURSE, IF SHE'D JUST TOLD ME HER SECRET, WE COULD HAVE AVOIDED THIS WHOLE ARENDELLE-IN-DEEP-WINTER THING.
WHOOSH
OOO!
WAIT! NO. COME BACK HERE! OKAY.
Forget the horse. Keep going.
SNOW. IT HAD TO BE SNOW. SHE COULDN'T HAVE TROPICAL MAGIC THAT COVERED THE FJORDS IN WHITE SAND AND WARM--
--FIRE! AH-HAH--
--HAAAAH--OOF!
A place to get some gear. Warm up. Take a breather.
Progress! You can do this, Anna.

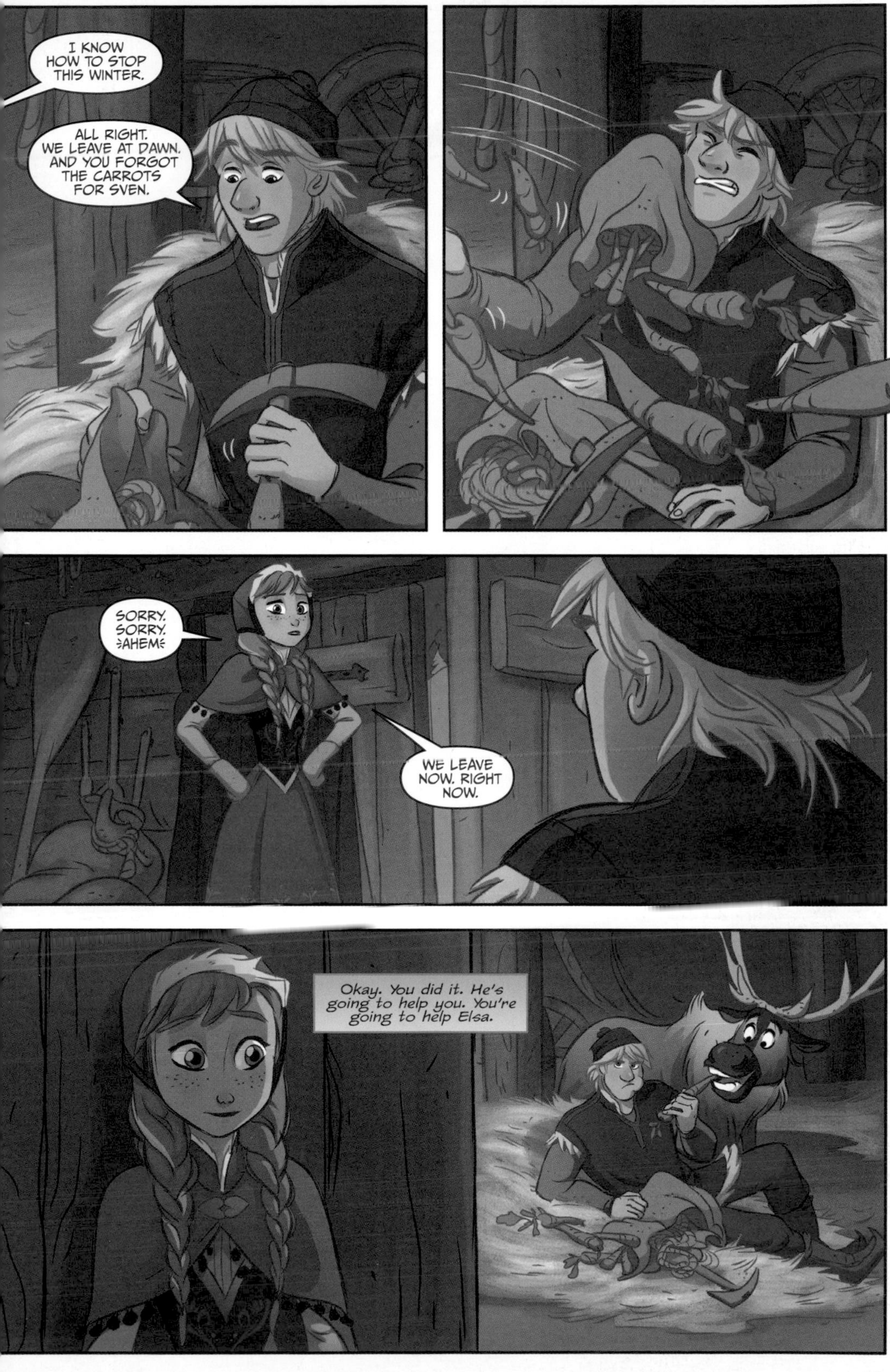
I KNOW HOW TO STOP THIS WINTER.
ALL RIGHT. WE LEAVE AT DAWN. AND YOU FORGOT THE CARROTS FOR SVEN.
SORRY. SORRY. AHEM
WE LEAVE NOW. RIGHT NOW.
Okay. You did it. He's going to help you. You're going to help Elsa.

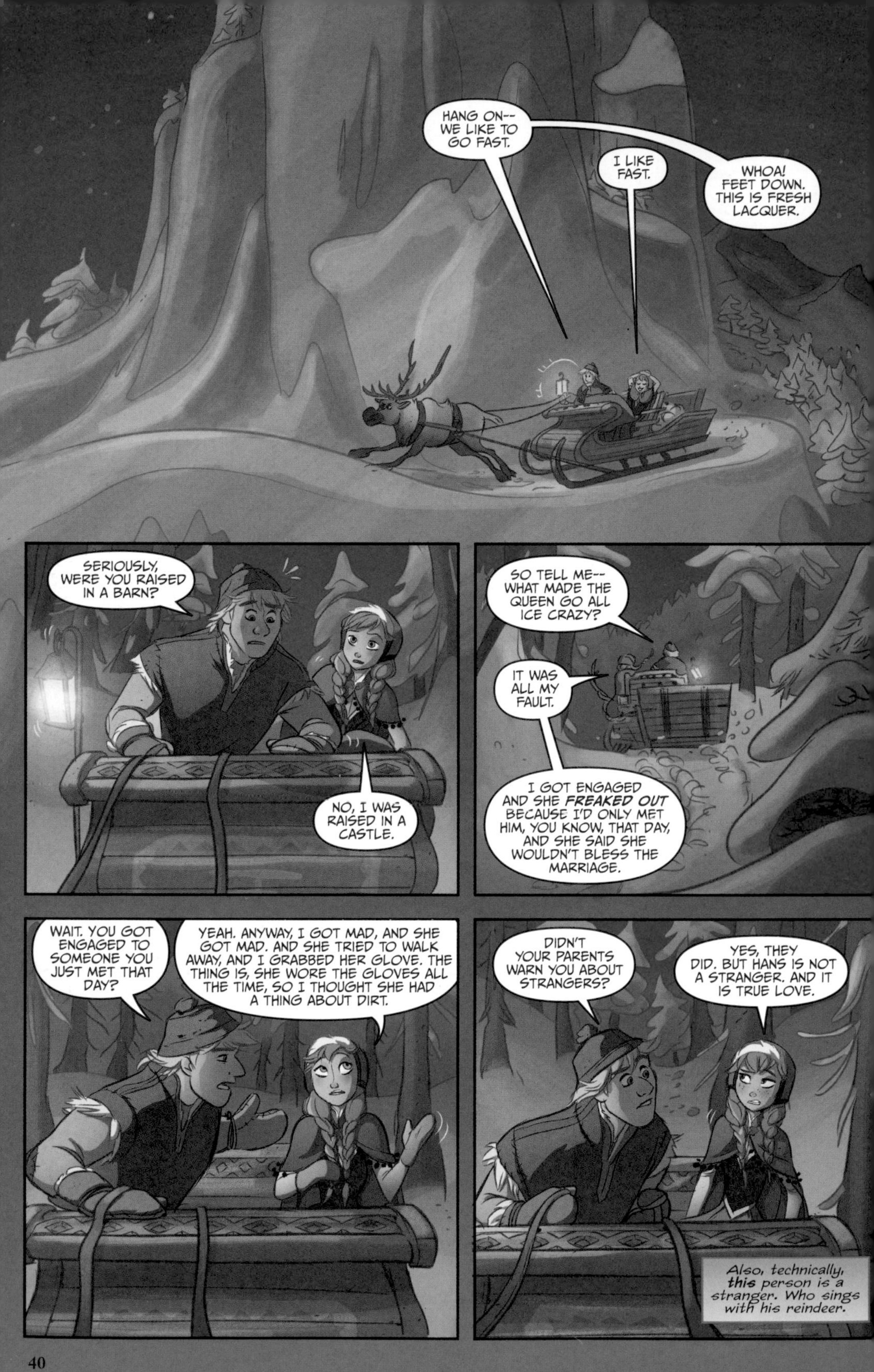
HANG ON--
WE LIKE TO
GO FAST.
I LIKE
FAST.
WHOA!
FEET DOWN.
THIS IS FRESH
LACQUER.
SERIOUSLY,
WERE YOU RAISED
IN A BARN?
NO, I WAS
RAISED IN A
CASTLE.
SO TELL ME--
WHAT MADE THE
QUEEN GO ALL
ICE CRAZY?
IT WAS
ALL MY
FAULT.
I GOT ENGAGED
AND SHE ***FREAKED OUT***
BECAUSE I'D ONLY MET
HIM, YOU KNOW, THAT DAY,
AND SHE SAID SHE
WOULDN'T BLESS THE
MARRIAGE.
WAIT. YOU GOT
ENGAGED TO
SOMEONE YOU
JUST MET THAT
DAY?
YEAH. ANYWAY, I GOT MAD, AND SHE
GOT MAD. AND SHE TRIED TO WALK
AWAY, AND I GRABBED HER GLOVE. THE
THING IS, SHE WORE THE GLOVES ALL
THE TIME, SO I THOUGHT SHE HAD
A THING ABOUT DIRT.
DIDN'T
YOUR PARENTS
WARN YOU ABOUT
STRANGERS?
YES, THEY
DID. BUT HANS IS NOT
A STRANGER. AND IT
IS TRUE LOVE.
Also, technically,
this *person is a*
stranger. Who sings
with his reindeer.

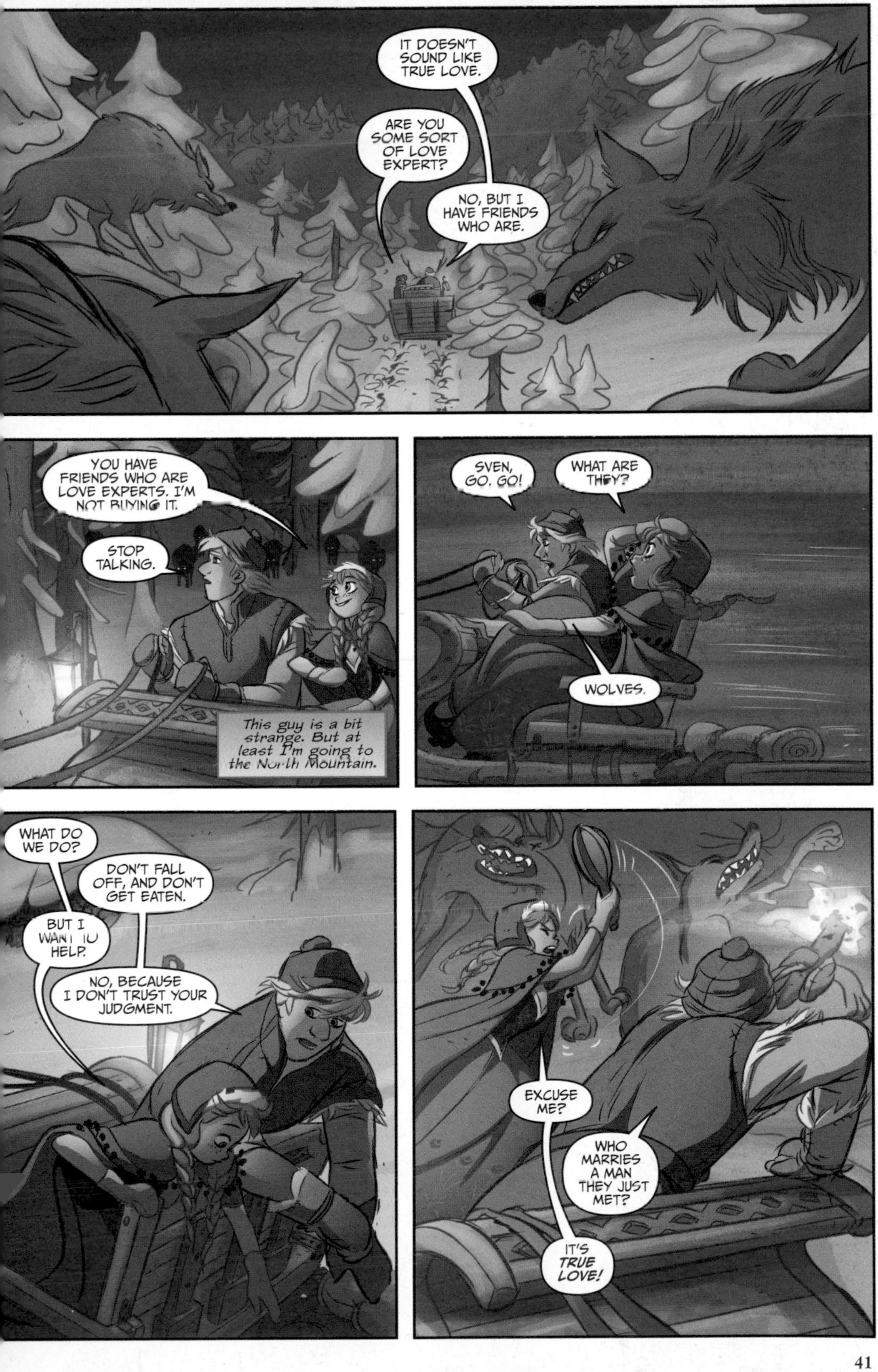
IT DOESN'T SOUND LIKE TRUE LOVE.
ARE YOU SOME SORT OF LOVE EXPERT?
NO, BUT I HAVE FRIENDS WHO ARE.
YOU HAVE FRIENDS WHO ARE LOVE EXPERTS. I'M NOT BUYING IT.
STOP TALKING.
This guy is a bit strange. But at least I'm going to the North Mountain.
SVEN, GO. GO!
WHAT ARE THEY?
WOLVES.
WHAT DO WE DO?
DON'T FALL OFF, AND DON'T GET EATEN.
BUT I WANT TO HELP.
NO, BECAUSE I DON'T TRUST YOUR JUDGMENT.
EXCUSE ME?
WHO MARRIES A MAN THEY JUST MET?
IT'S *TRUE LOVE!*

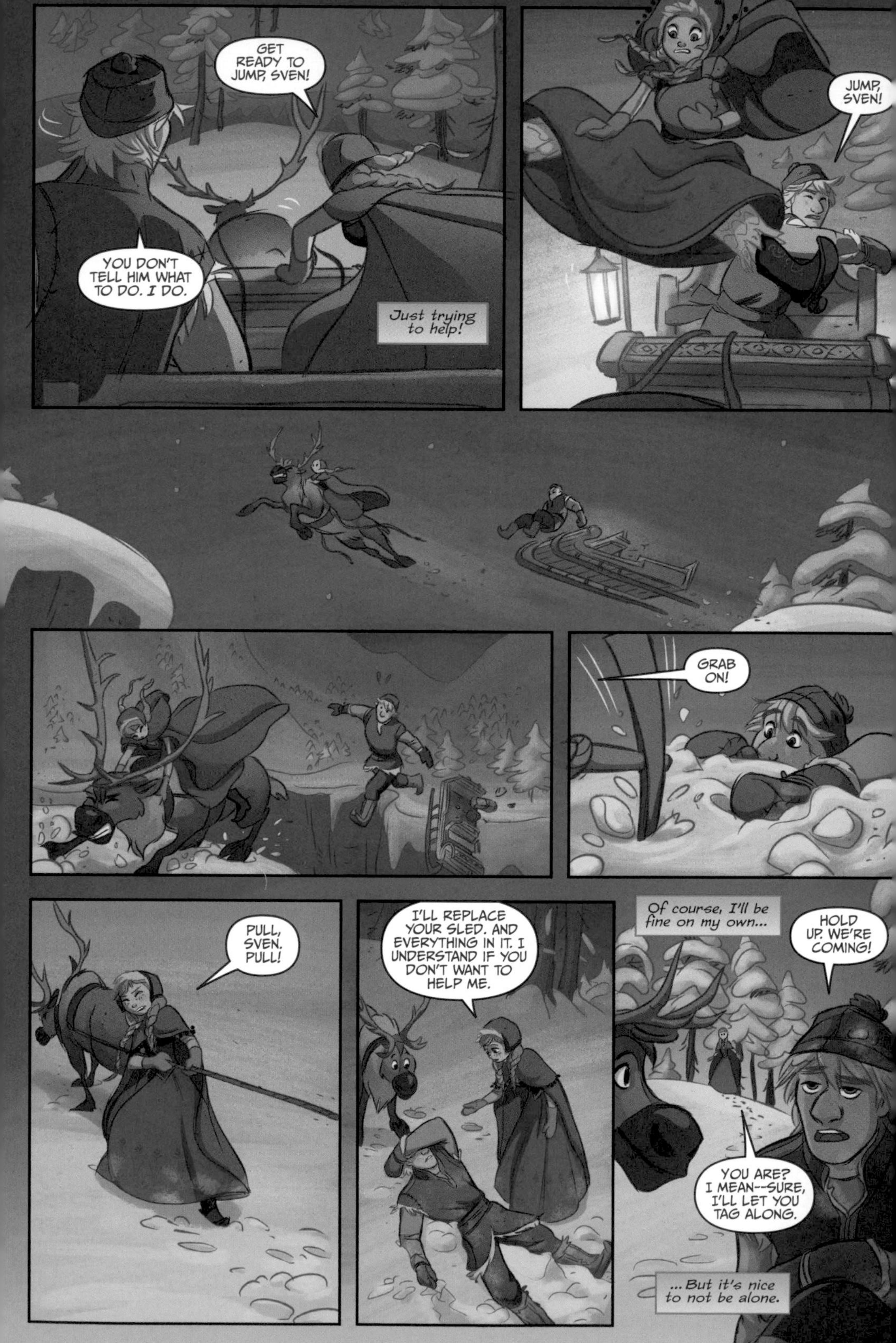
GET READY TO JUMP, SVEN!
YOU DON'T TELL HIM WHAT TO DO. I DO.
Just trying to help!
JUMP, SVEN!
GRAB ON!
PULL, SVEN. PULL!
I'LL REPLACE YOUR SLED. AND EVERYTHING IN IT. I UNDERSTAND IF YOU DON'T WANT TO HELP ME.
Of course, I'll be fine on my own...
HOLD UP. WE'RE COMING!
YOU ARE? I MEAN--SURE, I'LL LET YOU TAG ALONG.
...But it's nice to not be alone.

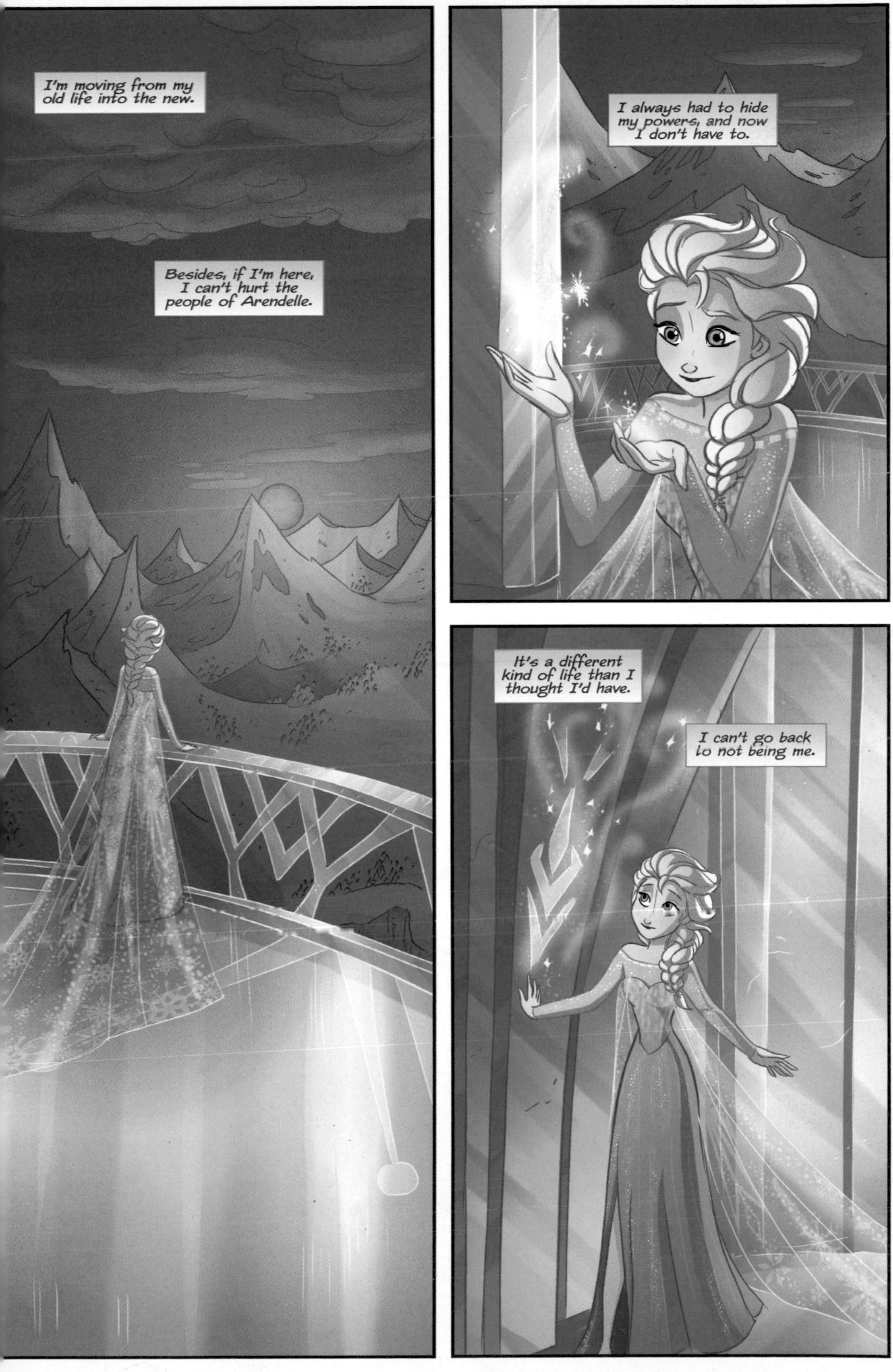
I'm moving from my old life into the new.
Besides, if I'm here, I can't hurt the people of Arendelle.
I always had to hide my powers, and now I don't have to.
It's a different kind of life than I thought I'd have.
I can't go back to not being me.

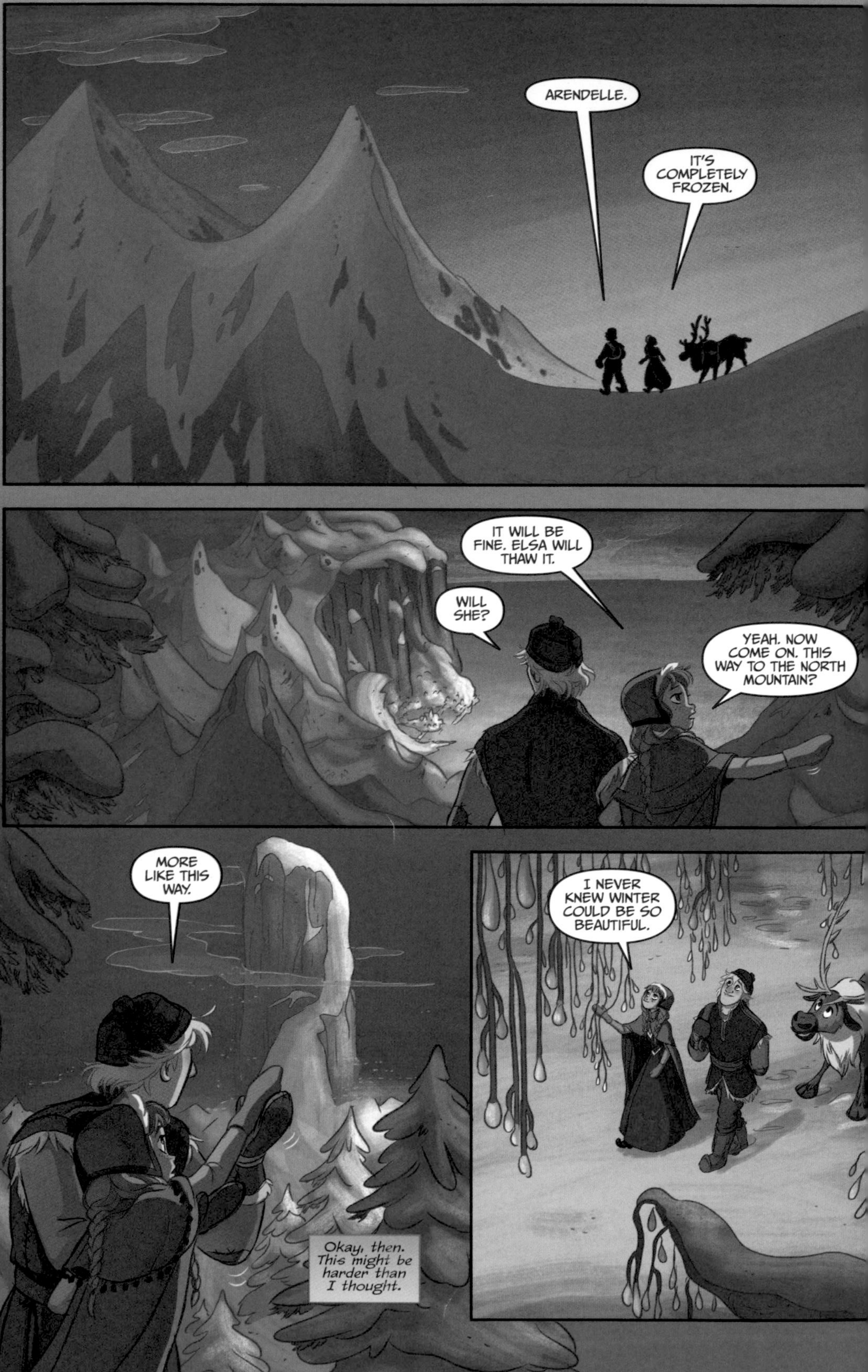
ARENDELLE.
IT'S COMPLETELY FROZEN.
IT WILL BE FINE. ELSA WILL THAW IT.
WILL SHE?
YEAH. NOW COME ON. THIS WAY TO THE NORTH MOUNTAIN?
MORE LIKE THIS WAY.
Okay, then. This might be harder than I thought.
I NEVER KNEW WINTER COULD BE SO BEAUTIFUL.

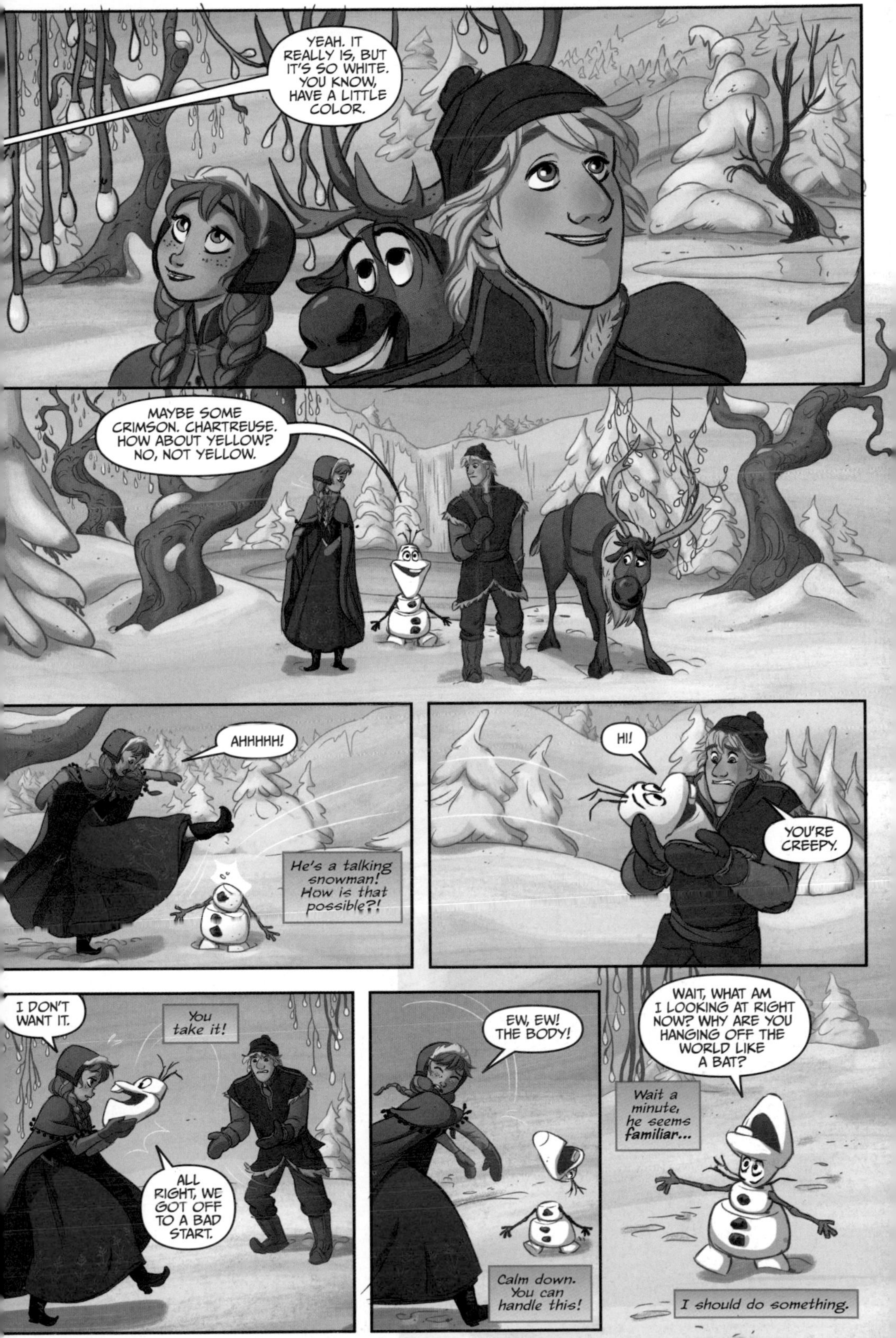

YEAH. IT REALLY IS, BUT IT'S SO WHITE. YOU KNOW, HAVE A LITTLE COLOR.
MAYBE SOME CRIMSON. CHARTREUSE. HOW ABOUT YELLOW? NO, NOT YELLOW.
AHHHHH!
He's a talking snowman! How is that possible?!
HI!
YOU'RE CREEPY.
I DON'T WANT IT.
You take it!
ALL RIGHT, WE GOT OFF TO A BAD START.
EW, EW! THE BODY!
Calm down. You can handle this!
WAIT, WHAT AM I LOOKING AT RIGHT NOW? WHY ARE YOU HANGING OFF THE WORLD LIKE A BAT?
Wait a minute, he seems **familiar...**
I should do something.

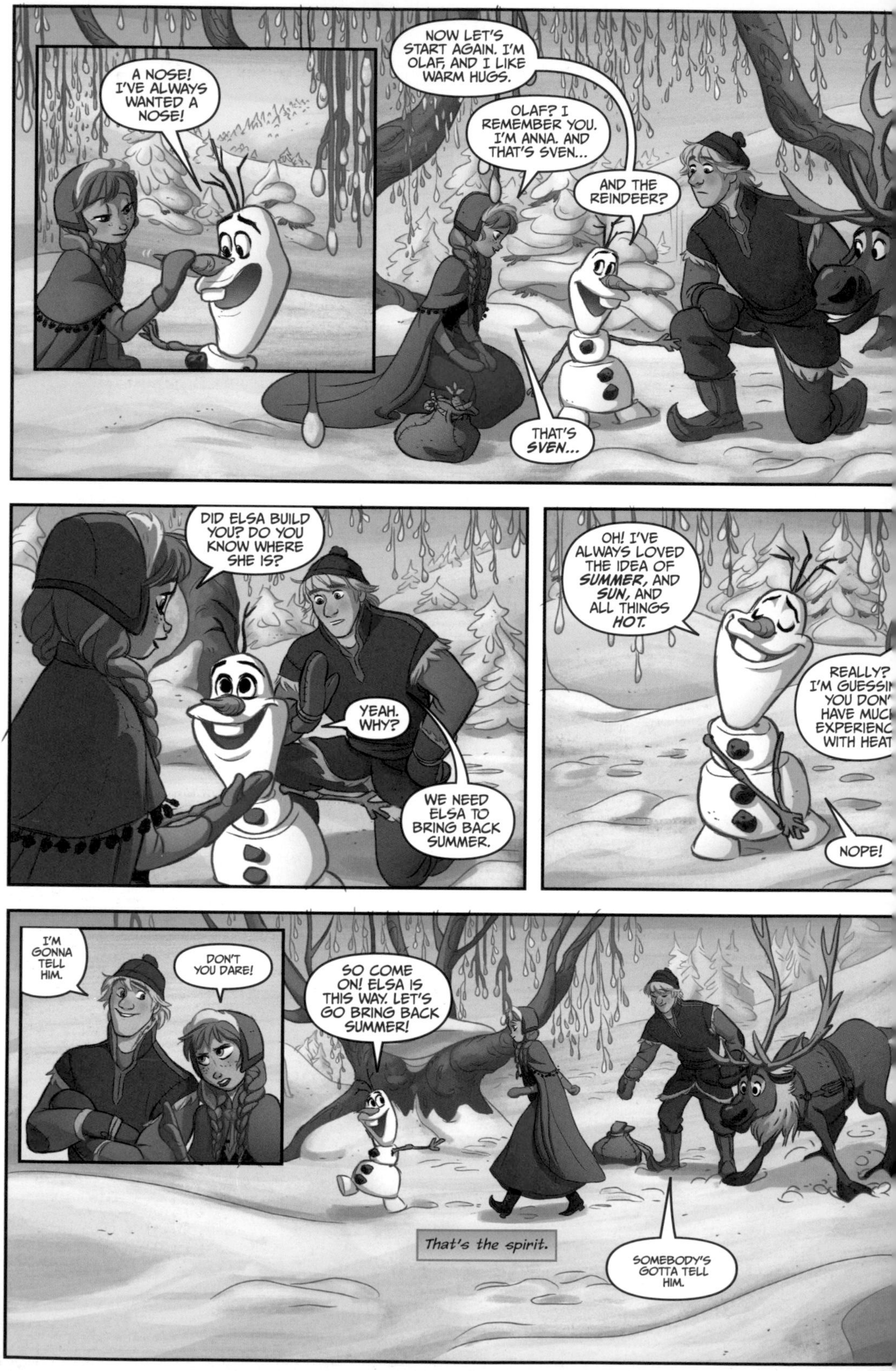
A NOSE! I'VE ALWAYS WANTED A NOSE!
NOW LET'S START AGAIN. I'M OLAF, AND I LIKE WARM HUGS.
OLAF? I REMEMBER YOU. I'M ANNA. AND THAT'S SVEN...
AND THE REINDEER?
THAT'S SVEN...
DID ELSA BUILD YOU? DO YOU KNOW WHERE SHE IS?
YEAH. WHY?
WE NEED ELSA TO BRING BACK SUMMER.
OH! I'VE ALWAYS LOVED THE IDEA OF SUMMER, AND SUN, AND ALL THINGS HOT.
REALLY? I'M GUESSI YOU DON' HAVE MUC EXPERIENC WITH HEAT
NOPE!
I'M GONNA TELL HIM.
DON'T YOU DARE!
SO COME ON! ELSA IS THIS WAY. LET'S GO BRING BACK SUMMER!
That's the spirit.
SOMEBODY'S GOTTA TELL HIM.

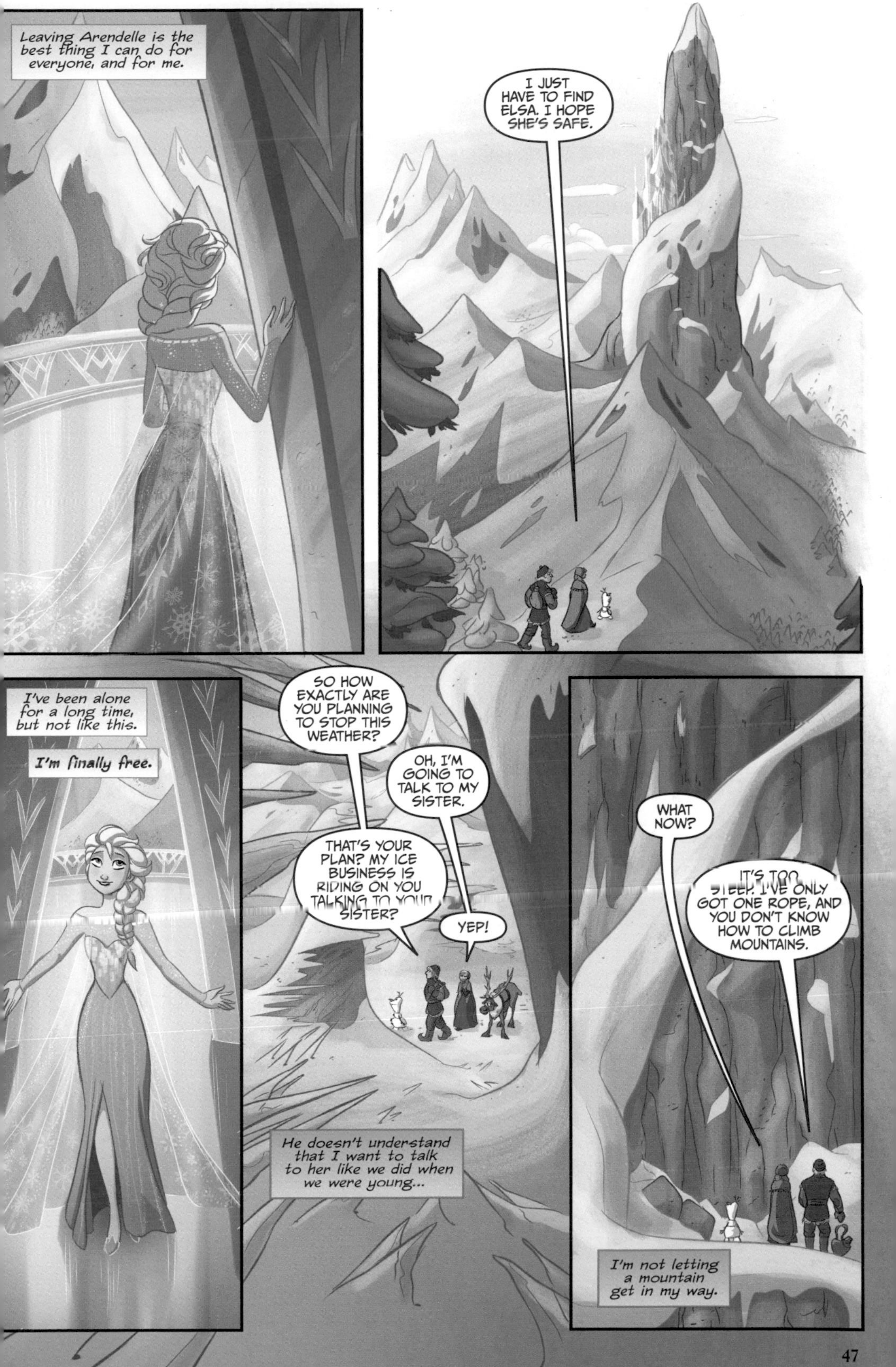
Leaving Arendelle is the best thing I can do for everyone, and for me.
I JUST HAVE TO FIND ELSA. I HOPE SHE'S SAFE.
I've been alone for a long time, but not like this.
I'm finally free.
SO HOW EXACTLY ARE YOU PLANNING TO STOP THIS WEATHER?
OH, I'M GOING TO TALK TO MY SISTER.
THAT'S YOUR PLAN? MY ICE BUSINESS IS RIDING ON YOU TALKING TO YOUR SISTER?
YEP!
He doesn't understand that I want to talk to her like we did when we were young...
WHAT NOW?
IT'S TOO STEEP. I'VE ONLY GOT ONE ROPE, AND YOU DON'T KNOW HOW TO CLIMB MOUNTAINS.
I'm not letting a mountain get in my way.

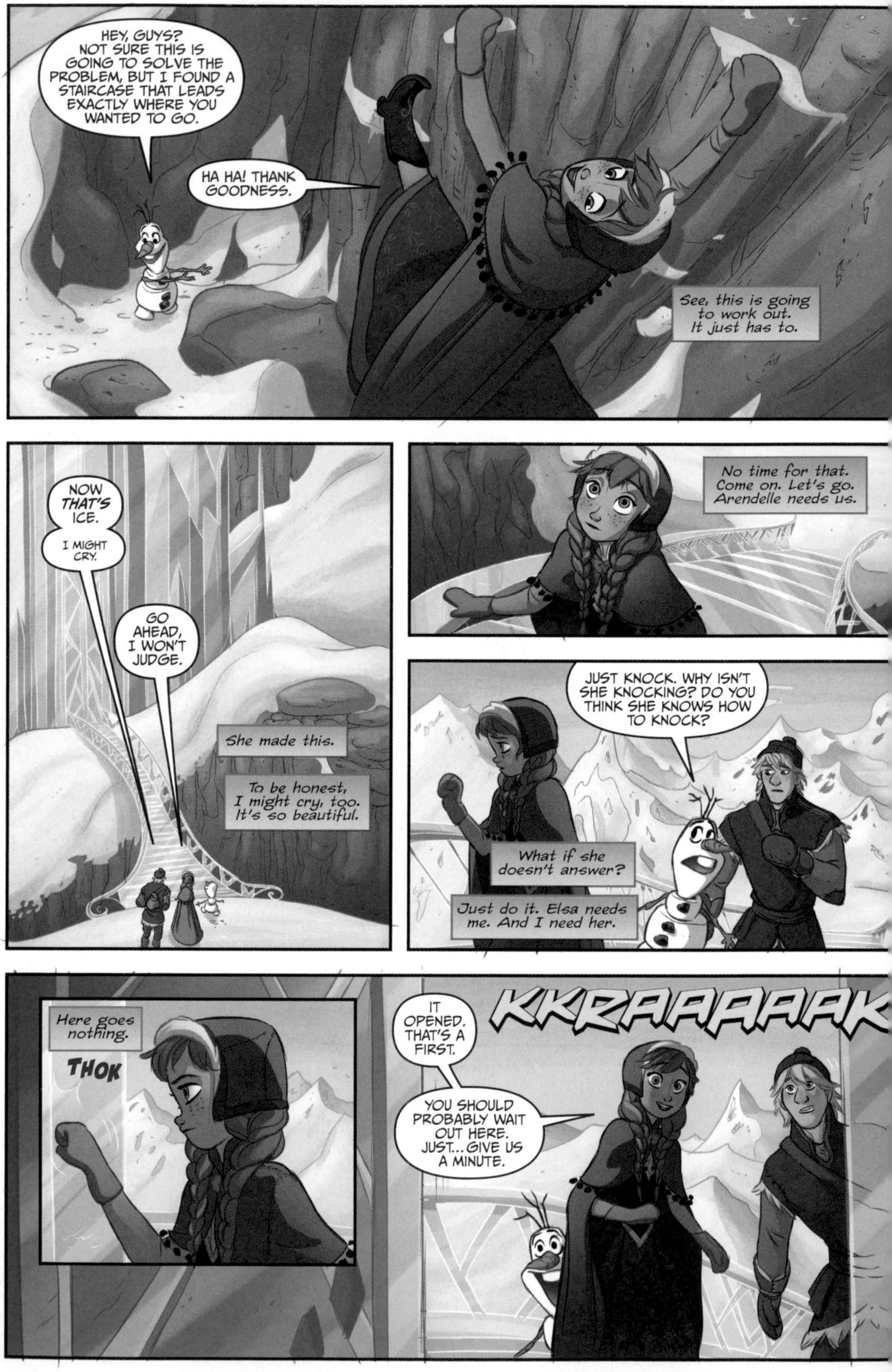
HEY, GUYS? NOT SURE THIS IS GOING TO SOLVE THE PROBLEM, BUT I FOUND A STAIRCASE THAT LEADS EXACTLY WHERE YOU WANTED TO GO.
HA HA! THANK GOODNESS.
See, this is going to work out. It just has to.
NOW *THAT'S* ICE.
I MIGHT CRY.
GO AHEAD, I WON'T JUDGE.
She made this.
To be honest, I might cry, too. It's so beautiful.
No time for that. Come on. Let's go. Arendelle needs us.
JUST KNOCK. WHY ISN'T SHE KNOCKING? DO YOU THINK SHE KNOWS HOW TO KNOCK?
What if she doesn't answer?
Just do it. Elsa needs me. And I need her.
Here goes nothing.
THOK
KKRAAAAAAK
IT OPENED. THAT'S A FIRST.
YOU SHOULD PROBABLY WAIT OUT HERE. JUST...GIVE US A MINUTE.

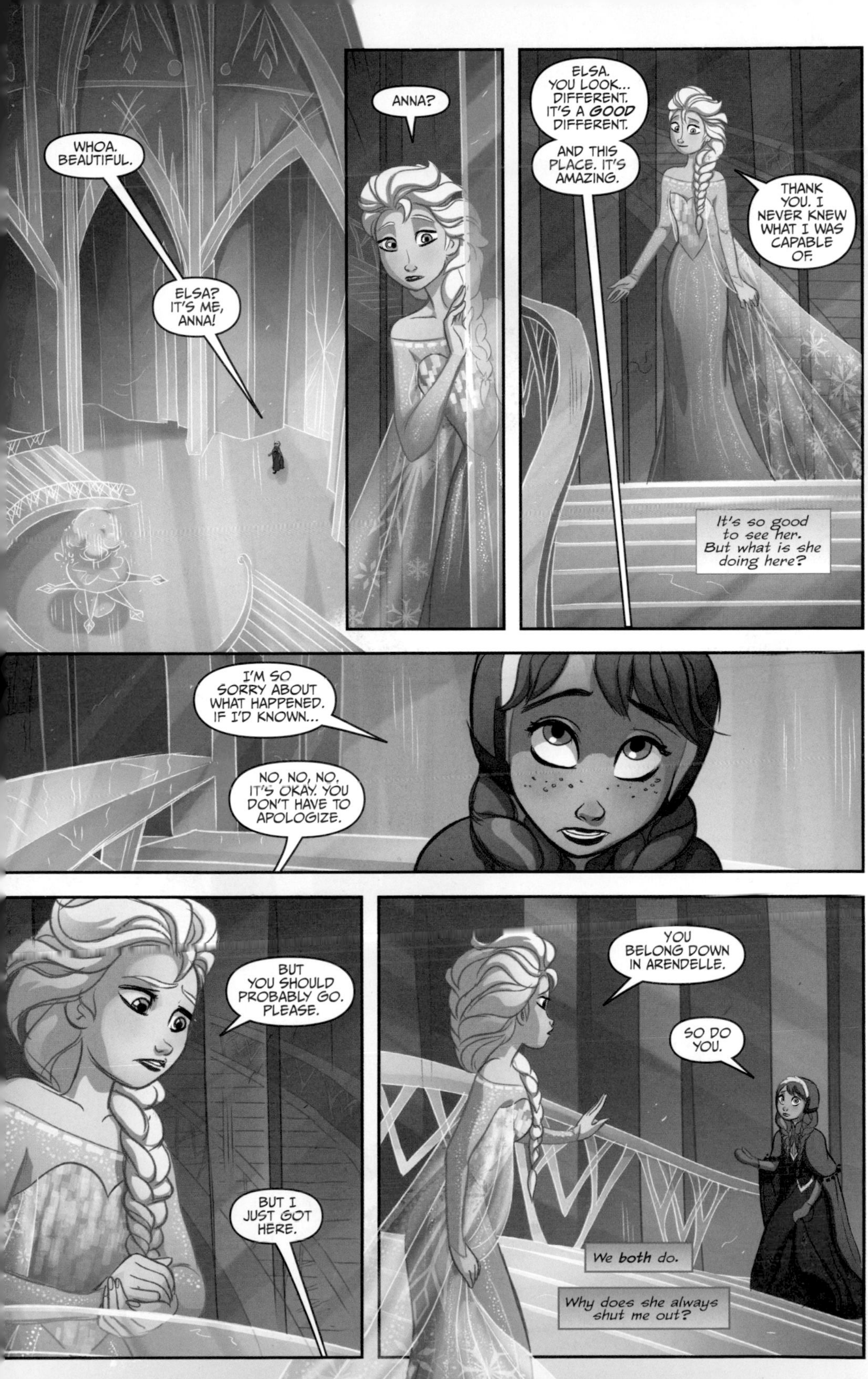
WHOA. BEAUTIFUL.
ELSA? IT'S ME, ANNA!
ANNA?
ELSA. YOU LOOK... DIFFERENT. IT'S A GOOD DIFFERENT.
AND THIS PLACE. IT'S AMAZING.
THANK YOU. I NEVER KNEW WHAT I WAS CAPABLE OF.
It's so good to see her. But what is she doing here?
I'M SO SORRY ABOUT WHAT HAPPENED. IF I'D KNOWN...
NO, NO, NO. IT'S OKAY. YOU DON'T HAVE TO APOLOGIZE.
BUT YOU SHOULD PROBABLY GO. PLEASE.
BUT I JUST GOT HERE.
YOU BELONG DOWN IN ARENDELLE.
SO DO YOU.
We both do.
Why does she always shut me out?

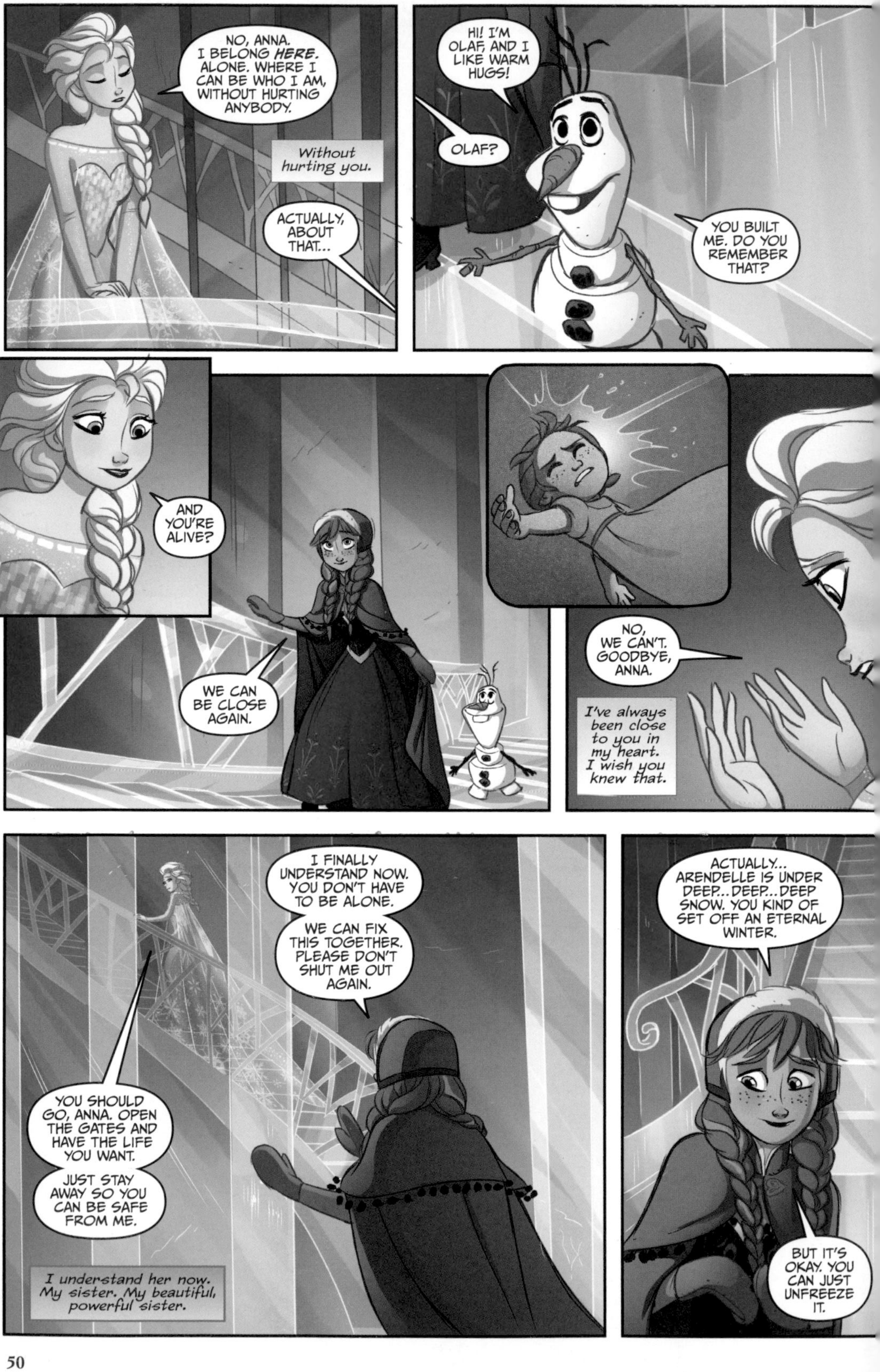
NO, ANNA. I BELONG **HERE**. ALONE. WHERE I CAN BE WHO I AM, WITHOUT HURTING ANYBODY.
Without hurting you.
ACTUALLY, ABOUT THAT...
HI! I'M OLAF, AND I LIKE WARM HUGS!
OLAF?
YOU BUILT ME. DO YOU REMEMBER THAT?
AND YOU'RE ALIVE?
WE CAN BE CLOSE AGAIN.
NO, WE CAN'T. GOODBYE, ANNA.
I've always been close to you in my heart. I wish you knew that.
I FINALLY UNDERSTAND NOW. YOU DON'T HAVE TO BE ALONE.
WE CAN FIX THIS TOGETHER. PLEASE DON'T SHUT ME OUT AGAIN.
YOU SHOULD GO, ANNA. OPEN THE GATES AND HAVE THE LIFE YOU WANT.
JUST STAY AWAY SO YOU CAN BE SAFE FROM ME.
I understand her now. My sister. My beautiful, powerful sister.
ACTUALLY... ARENDELLE IS UNDER DEEP...DEEP...DEEP SNOW. YOU KIND OF SET OFF AN ETERNAL WINTER.
BUT IT'S OKAY. YOU CAN JUST UNFREEZE IT.

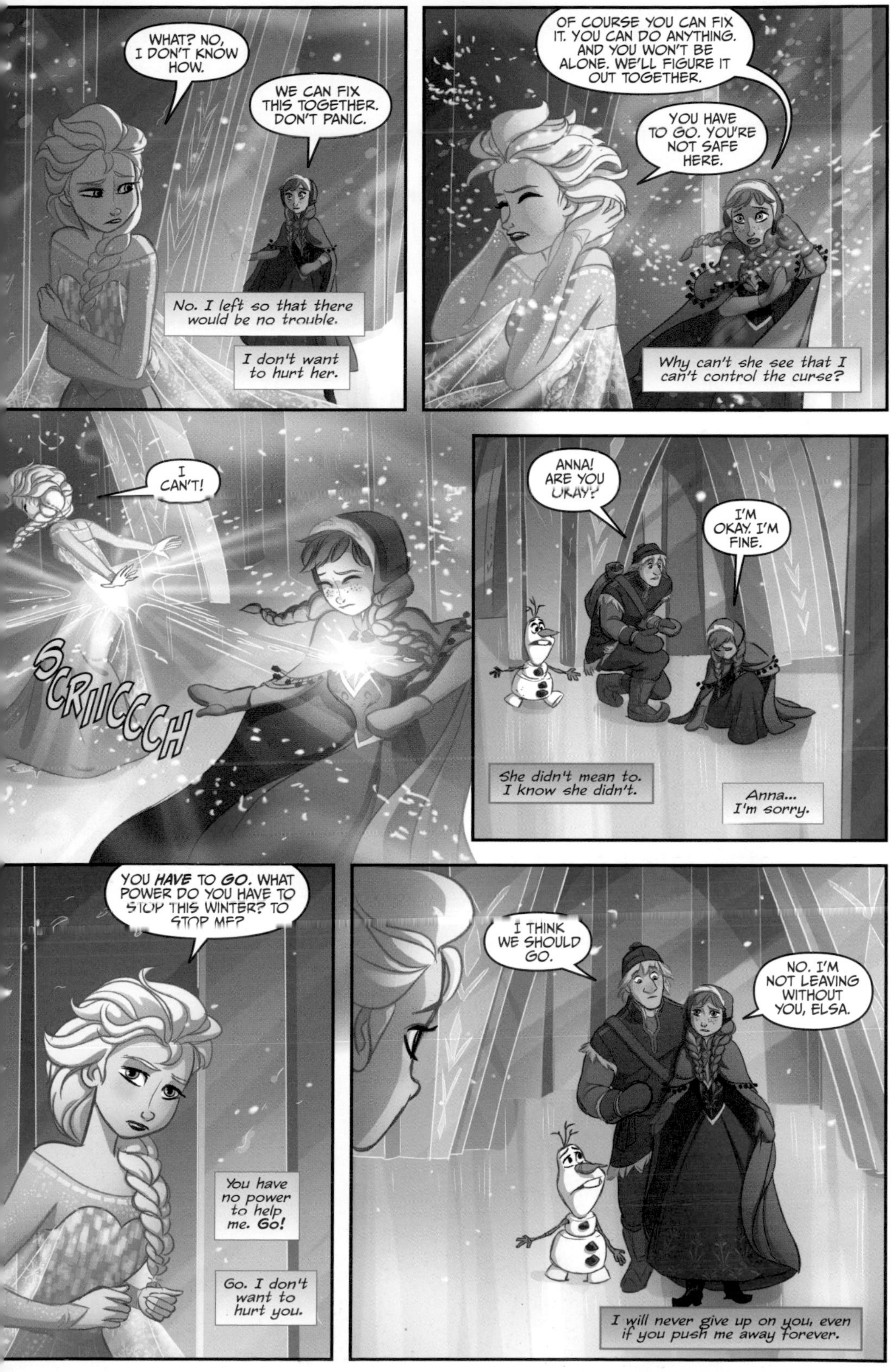
WHAT? NO, I DON'T KNOW HOW.
WE CAN FIX THIS TOGETHER. DON'T PANIC.
No. I left so that there would be no trouble.
I don't want to hurt her.
OF COURSE YOU CAN FIX IT. YOU CAN DO ANYTHING. AND YOU WON'T BE ALONE. WE'LL FIGURE IT OUT TOGETHER.
YOU HAVE TO GO. YOU'RE NOT SAFE HERE.
Why can't she see that I can't control the curse?
I CAN'T!
SCRIICCCH
ANNA! ARE YOU OKAY?
I'M OKAY. I'M FINE.
She didn't mean to. I know she didn't.
Anna... I'm sorry.
YOU *HAVE* TO *GO*. WHAT POWER DO YOU HAVE TO STOP THIS WINTER? TO STOP ME?
You have no power to help me. **Go!**
Go. I don't want to hurt you.
I THINK WE SHOULD GO.
NO. I'M NOT LEAVING WITHOUT YOU, ELSA.
I will never give up on you, even if you push me away forever.

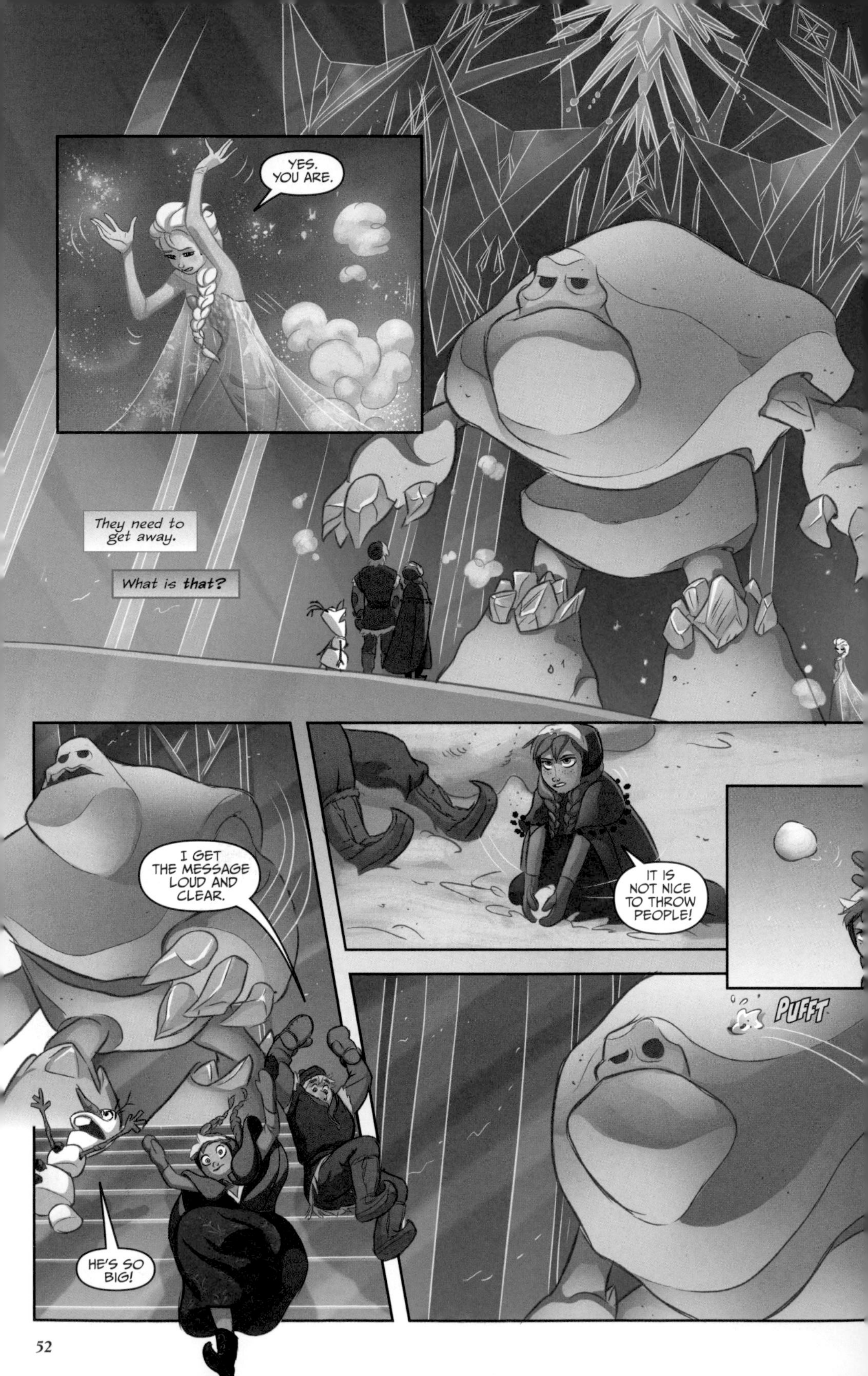
YES. YOU ARE.
They need to get away.
What is *that?*
I GET THE MESSAGE LOUD AND CLEAR.
HE'S SO BIG!
IT IS NOT NICE TO THROW PEOPLE!
PUFFT

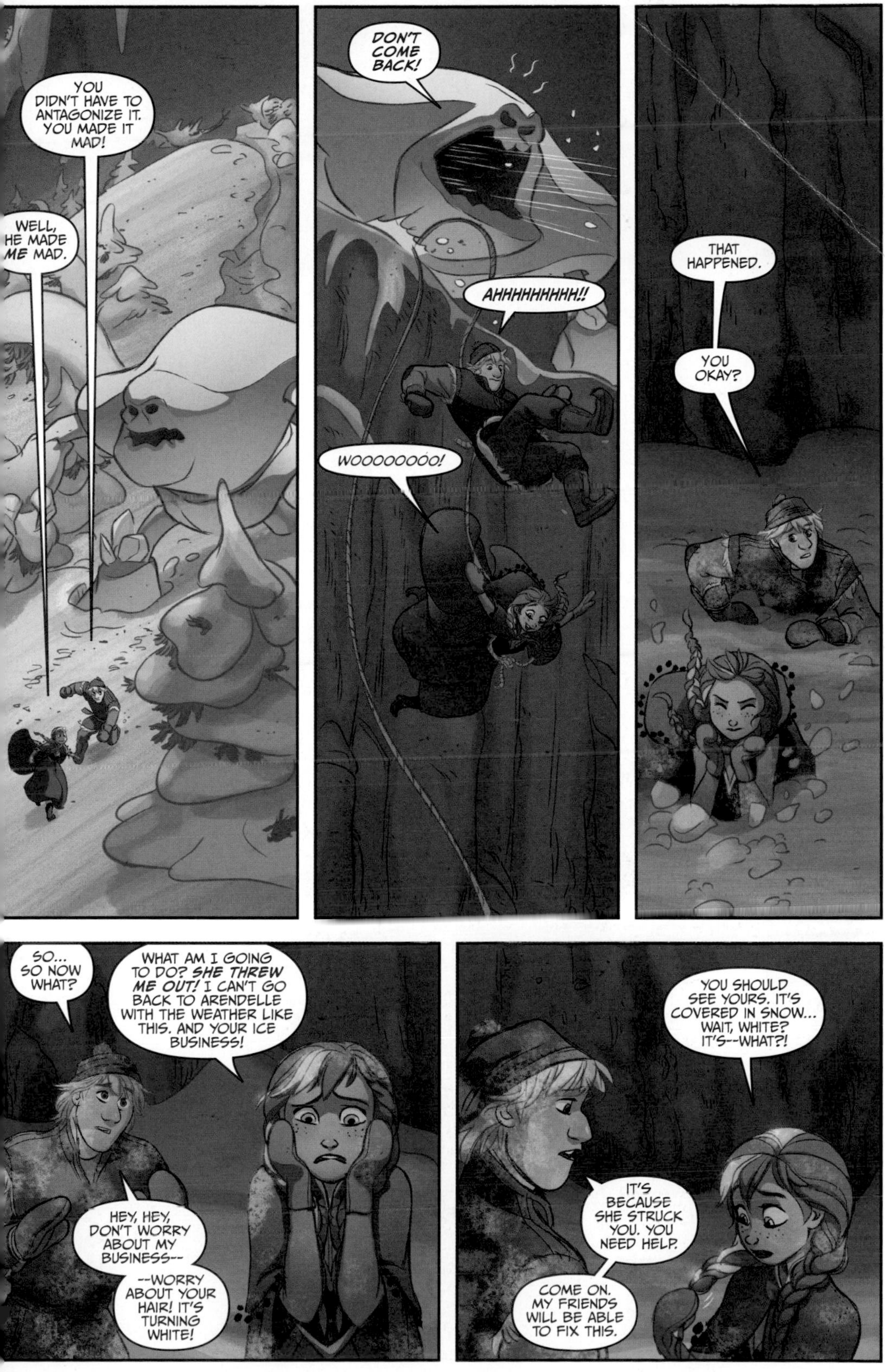
YOU DIDN'T HAVE TO ANTAGONIZE IT. YOU MADE IT MAD!
WELL, HE MADE ME MAD.
DON'T COME BACK!
AHHHHHHHHH!!
WOOOOOOOO!
THAT HAPPENED.
YOU OKAY?
SO... SO NOW WHAT?
WHAT AM I GOING TO DO? SHE THREW ME OUT! I CAN'T GO BACK TO ARENDELLE WITH THE WEATHER LIKE THIS. AND YOUR ICE BUSINESS!
HEY, HEY, DON'T WORRY ABOUT MY BUSINESS--
--WORRY ABOUT YOUR HAIR! IT'S TURNING WHITE!
YOU SHOULD SEE YOURS. IT'S COVERED IN SNOW... WAIT, WHITE? IT'S--WHAT?!
IT'S BECAUSE SHE STRUCK YOU. YOU NEED HELP.
COME ON. MY FRIENDS WILL BE ABLE TO FIX THIS.

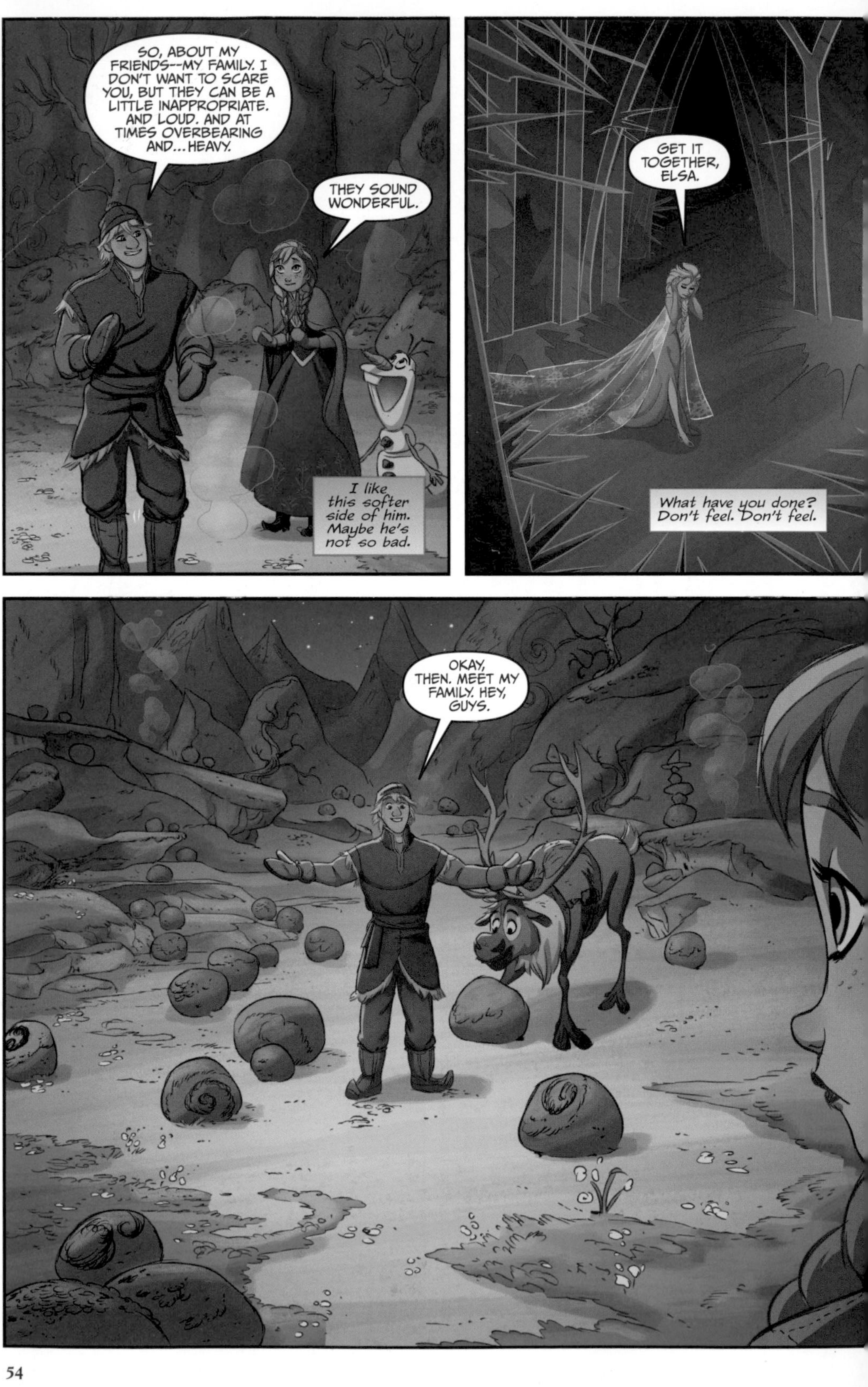
SO, ABOUT MY FRIENDS--MY FAMILY. I DON'T WANT TO SCARE YOU, BUT THEY CAN BE A LITTLE INAPPROPRIATE. AND LOUD. AND AT TIMES OVERBEARING AND... HEAVY.
THEY SOUND WONDERFUL.
I like this softer side of him. Maybe he's not so bad.
GET IT TOGETHER, ELSA.
What have you done? Don't feel. Don't feel.
OKAY, THEN. MEET MY FAMILY. HEY, GUYS.

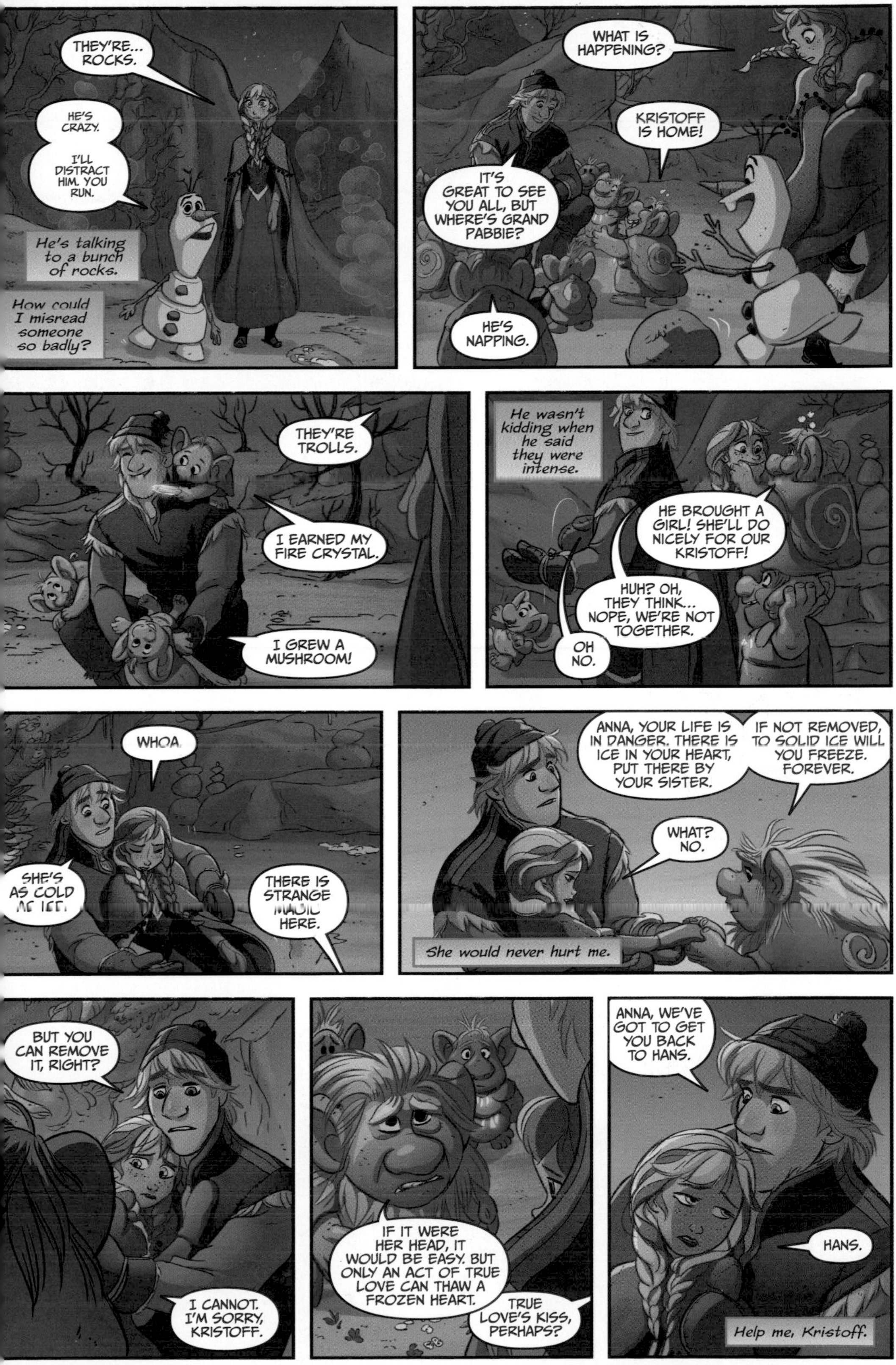

THEY'RE... ROCKS.
HE'S CRAZY.
I'LL DISTRACT HIM. YOU RUN.
He's talking to a bunch of rocks.
How could I misread someone so badly?
WHAT IS HAPPENING?
KRISTOFF IS HOME!
IT'S GREAT TO SEE YOU ALL, BUT WHERE'S GRAND PABBIE?
HE'S NAPPING.
THEY'RE TROLLS.
I EARNED MY FIRE CRYSTAL.
I GREW A MUSHROOM!
He wasn't kidding when he said they were intense.
HE BROUGHT A GIRL! SHE'LL DO NICELY FOR OUR KRISTOFF!
HUH? OH, THEY THINK... NOPE, WE'RE NOT TOGETHER.
OH NO.
WHOA.
SHE'S AS COLD
THERE IS STRANGE
HERE.
ANNA, YOUR LIFE IS IN DANGER. THERE IS ICE IN YOUR HEART, PUT THERE BY YOUR SISTER.
IF NOT REMOVED, TO SOLID ICE WILL YOU FREEZE. FOREVER.
WHAT? NO.
She would never hurt me.
BUT YOU CAN REMOVE IT, RIGHT?
I CANNOT. I'M SORRY, KRISTOFF.
IF IT WERE HER HEAD, IT WOULD BE EASY. BUT ONLY AN ACT OF TRUE LOVE CAN THAW A FROZEN HEART.
TRUE LOVE'S KISS, PERHAPS?
ANNA, WE'VE GOT TO GET YOU BACK TO HANS.
HANS.
Help me, Kristoff.

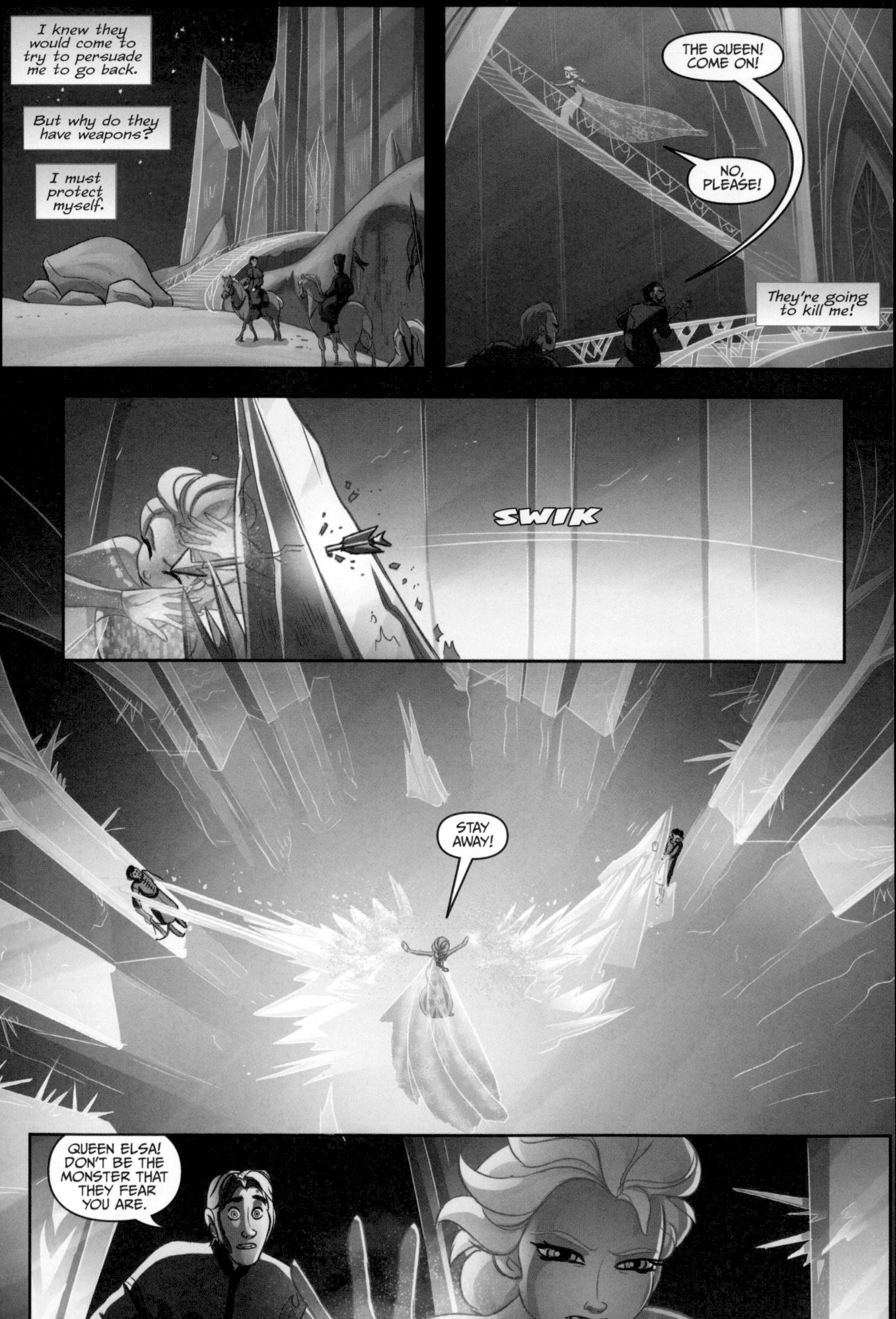
I knew they would come to try to persuade me to go back.
But why do they have weapons?
I must protect myself.
THE QUEEN! COME ON!
NO, PLEASE!
They're going to kill me!
SWIK
STAY AWAY!
QUEEN ELSA! DON'T BE THE MONSTER THAT THEY FEAR YOU ARE.

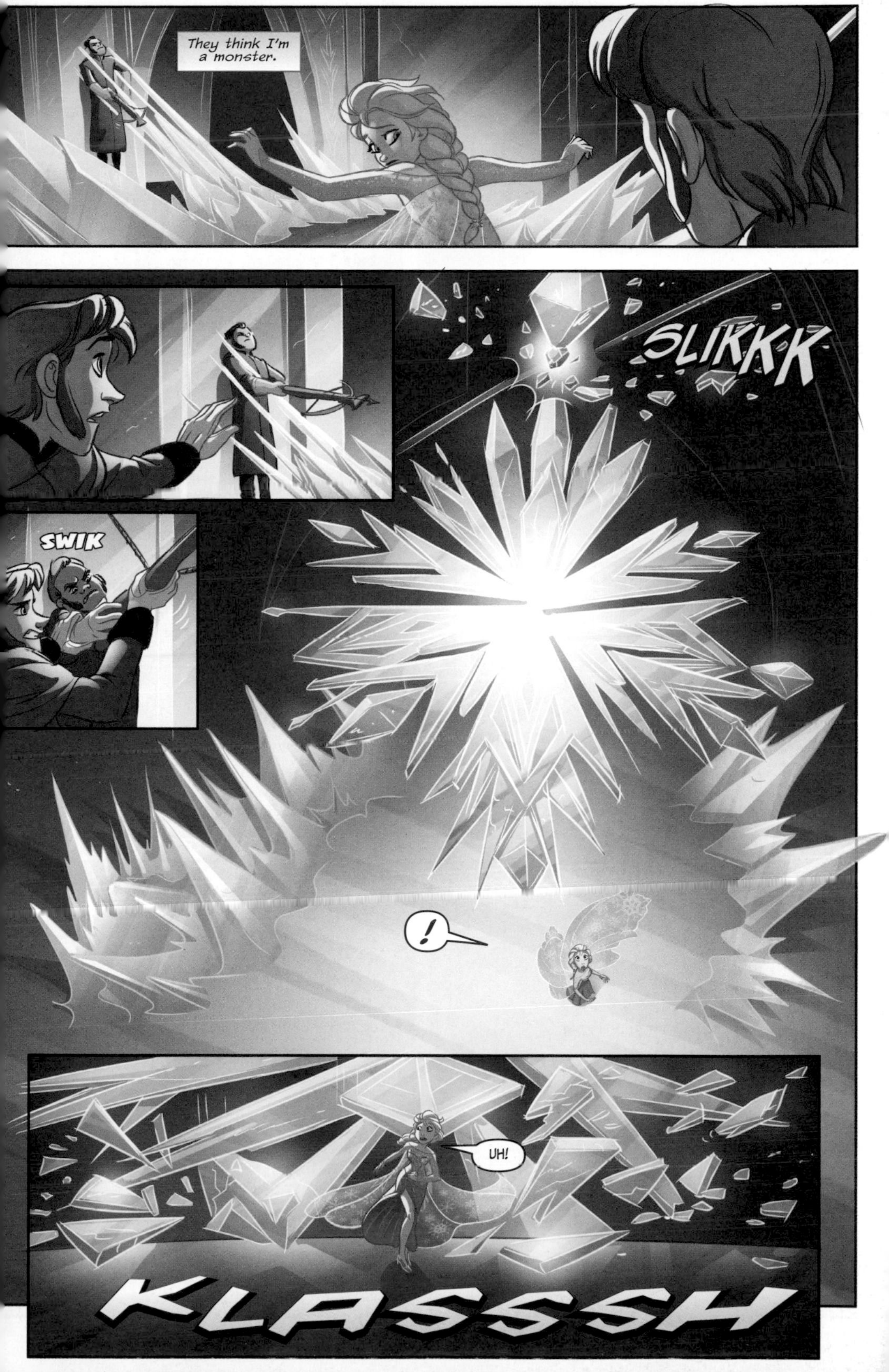
They think I'm a monster.
SLIKKK
SWIK
!
UH!
KLASSSH

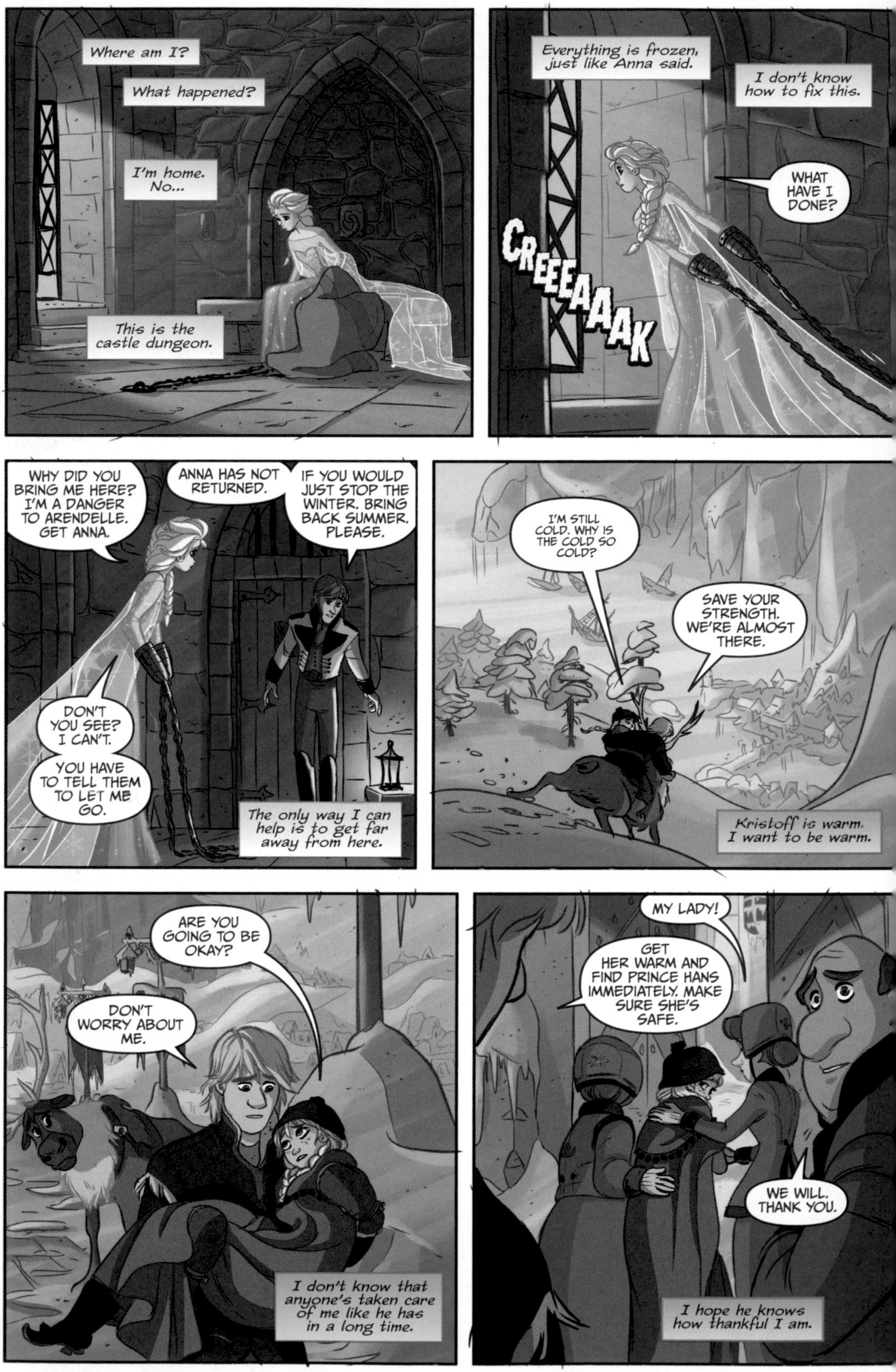

Where am I?
What happened?
I'm home. No...
This is the castle dungeon.
Everything is frozen, just like Anna said.
I don't know how to fix this.
WHAT HAVE I DONE?
CREEEAAAK
WHY DID YOU BRING ME HERE? I'M A DANGER TO ARENDELLE. GET ANNA.
ANNA HAS NOT RETURNED.
IF YOU WOULD JUST STOP THE WINTER. BRING BACK SUMMER. PLEASE.
DON'T YOU SEE? I CAN'T.
YOU HAVE TO TELL THEM TO LET ME GO.
The only way I can help is to get far away from here.
I'M STILL COLD. WHY IS THE COLD SO COLD?
SAVE YOUR STRENGTH. WE'RE ALMOST THERE.
Kristoff is warm. I want to be warm.
ARE YOU GOING TO BE OKAY?
DON'T WORRY ABOUT ME.
I don't know that anyone's taken care of me like he has in a long time.
MY LADY!
GET HER WARM AND FIND PRINCE HANS IMMEDIATELY. MAKE SURE SHE'S SAFE.
WE WILL. THANK YOU.
I hope he knows how thankful I am.

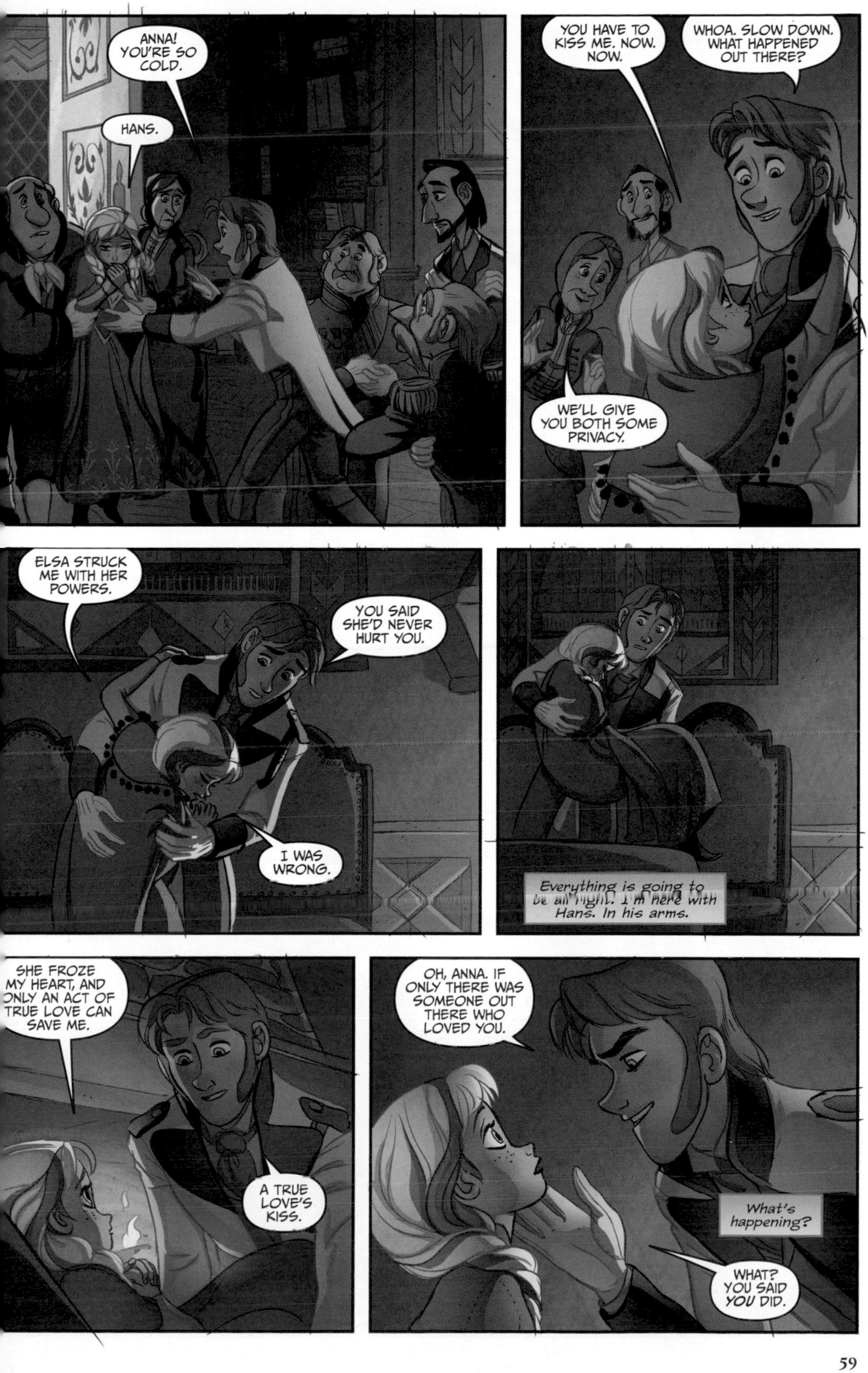
ANNA! YOU'RE SO COLD.
HANS.
YOU HAVE TO KISS ME. NOW. NOW.
WHOA. SLOW DOWN. WHAT HAPPENED OUT THERE?
WE'LL GIVE YOU BOTH SOME PRIVACY.
ELSA STRUCK ME WITH HER POWERS.
YOU SAID SHE'D NEVER HURT YOU.
I WAS WRONG.
Everything is going to be all right. I'm here with Hans. In his arms.
SHE FROZE MY HEART, AND ONLY AN ACT OF TRUE LOVE CAN SAVE ME.
A TRUE LOVE'S KISS.
OH, ANNA. IF ONLY THERE WAS SOMEONE OUT THERE WHO LOVED YOU.
What's happening?
WHAT? YOU SAID *YOU* DID.

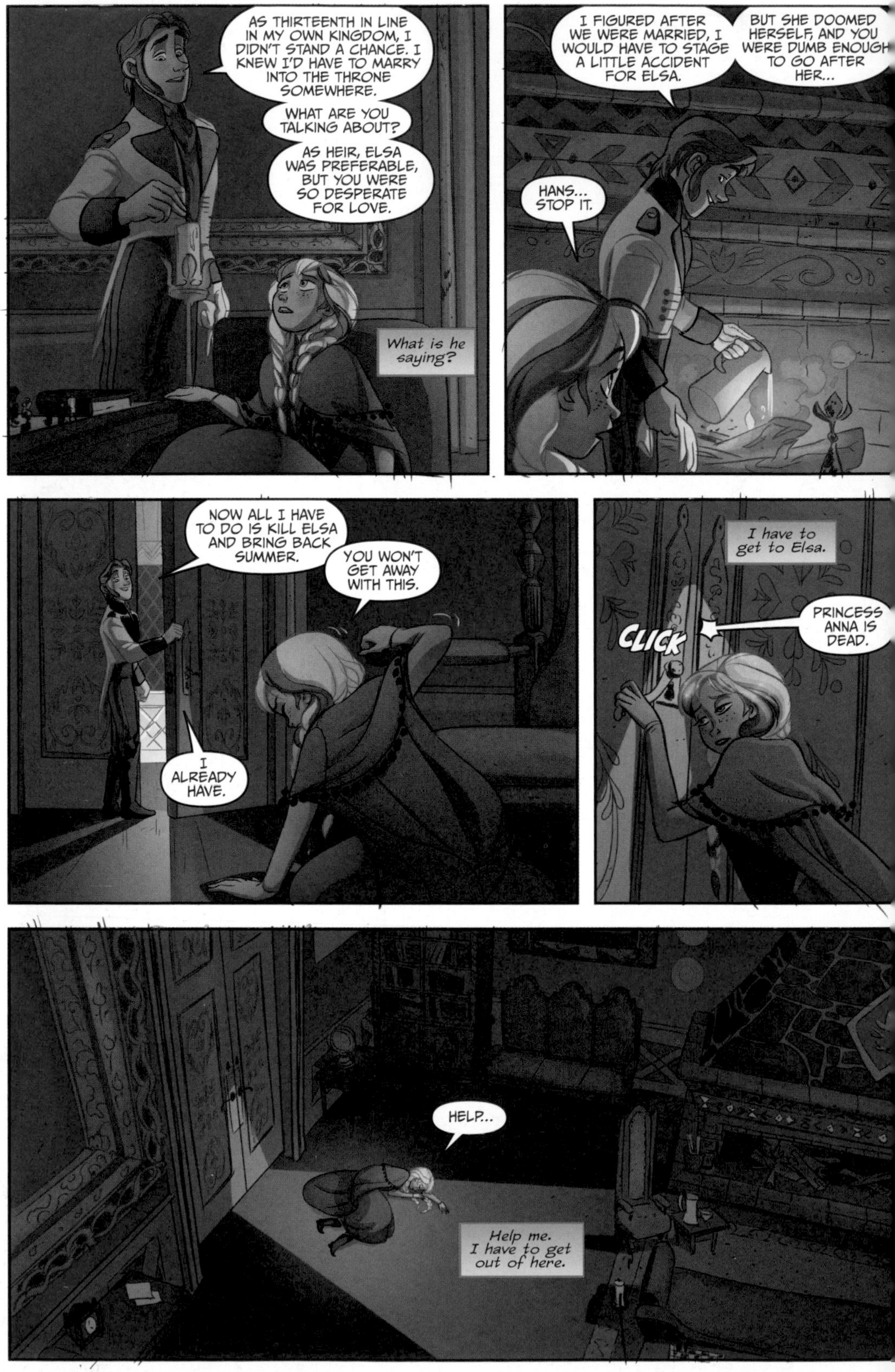
AS THIRTEENTH IN LINE IN MY OWN KINGDOM, I DIDN'T STAND A CHANCE. I KNEW I'D HAVE TO MARRY INTO THE THRONE SOMEWHERE.
WHAT ARE YOU TALKING ABOUT?
AS HEIR, ELSA WAS PREFERABLE, BUT YOU WERE SO DESPERATE FOR LOVE.
What is he saying?
I FIGURED AFTER WE WERE MARRIED, I WOULD HAVE TO STAGE A LITTLE ACCIDENT FOR ELSA.
BUT SHE DOOMED HERSELF, AND YOU WERE DUMB ENOUGH TO GO AFTER HER...
HANS... STOP IT.
NOW ALL I HAVE TO DO IS KILL ELSA AND BRING BACK SUMMER.
YOU WON'T GET AWAY WITH THIS.
I ALREADY HAVE.
I have to get to Elsa.
CLICK
PRINCESS ANNA IS DEAD.
HELP...
Help me. I have to get out of here.

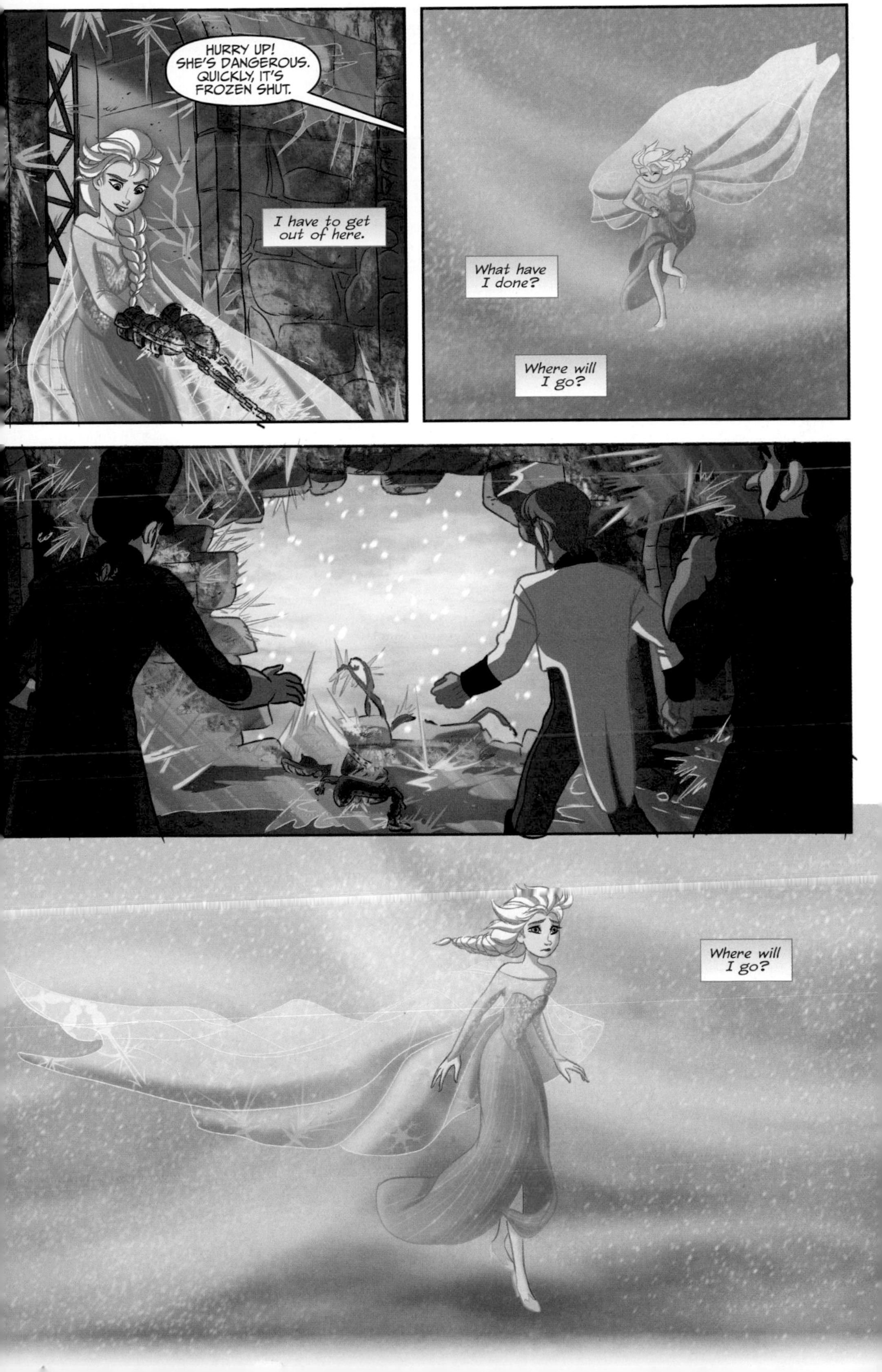
HURRY UP! SHE'S DANGEROUS. QUICKLY, IT'S FROZEN SHUT.
I have to get out of here.
What have I done?
Where will I go?
Where will I go?

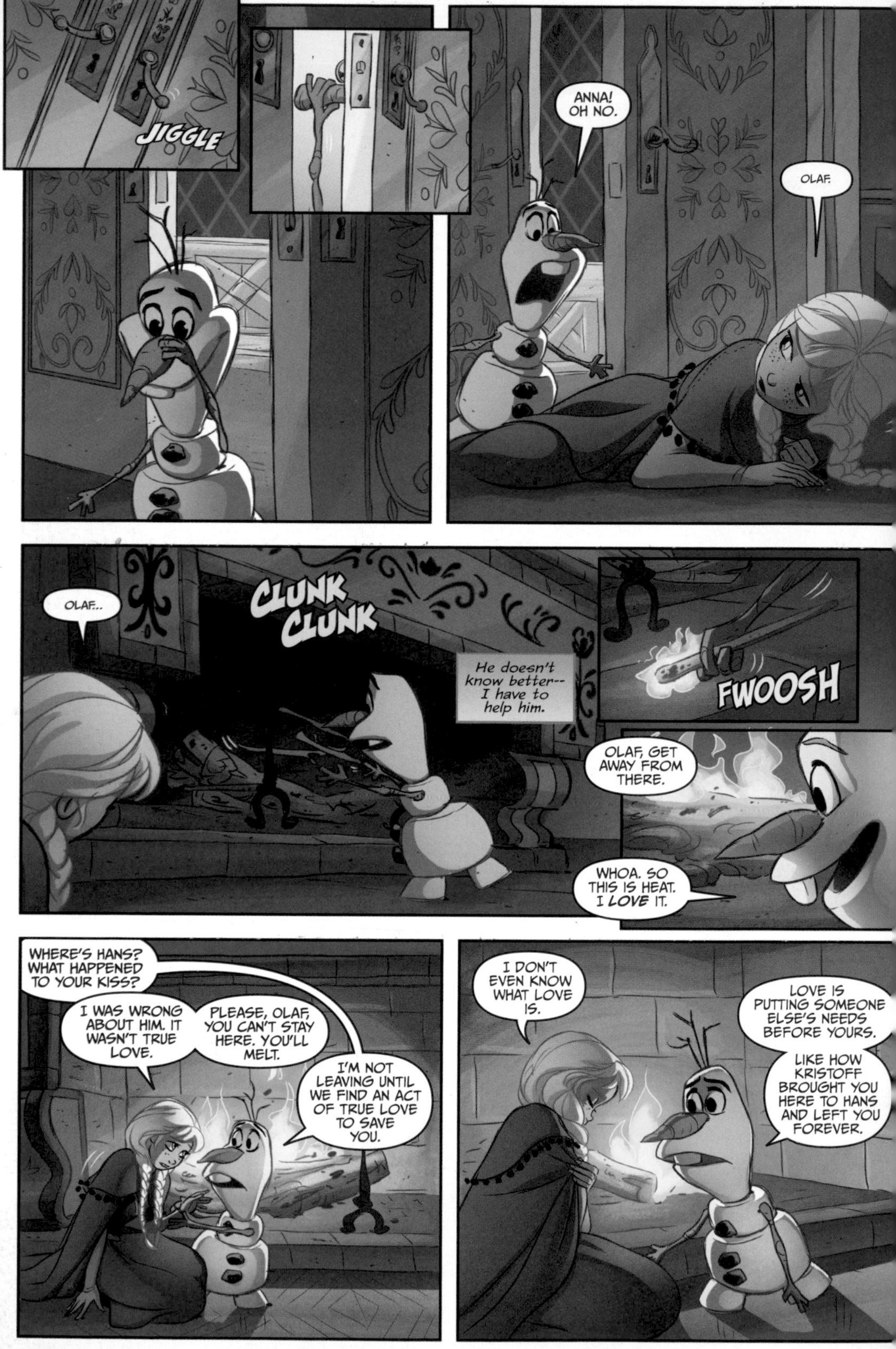
JIGGLE
ANNA! OH NO.
OLAF.
OLAF...
CLUNK CLUNK
He doesn't know better-- I have to help him.
FWOOSH
OLAF, GET AWAY FROM THERE.
WHOA. SO THIS IS HEAT. I LOVE IT.
WHERE'S HANS? WHAT HAPPENED TO YOUR KISS?
I WAS WRONG ABOUT HIM. IT WASN'T TRUE LOVE.
PLEASE, OLAF, YOU CAN'T STAY HERE. YOU'LL MELT.
I'M NOT LEAVING UNTIL WE FIND AN ACT OF TRUE LOVE TO SAVE YOU.
I DON'T EVEN KNOW WHAT LOVE IS.
LOVE IS PUTTING SOMEONE ELSE'S NEEDS BEFORE YOURS.
LIKE HOW KRISTOFF BROUGHT YOU HERE TO HANS AND LEFT YOU FOREVER.

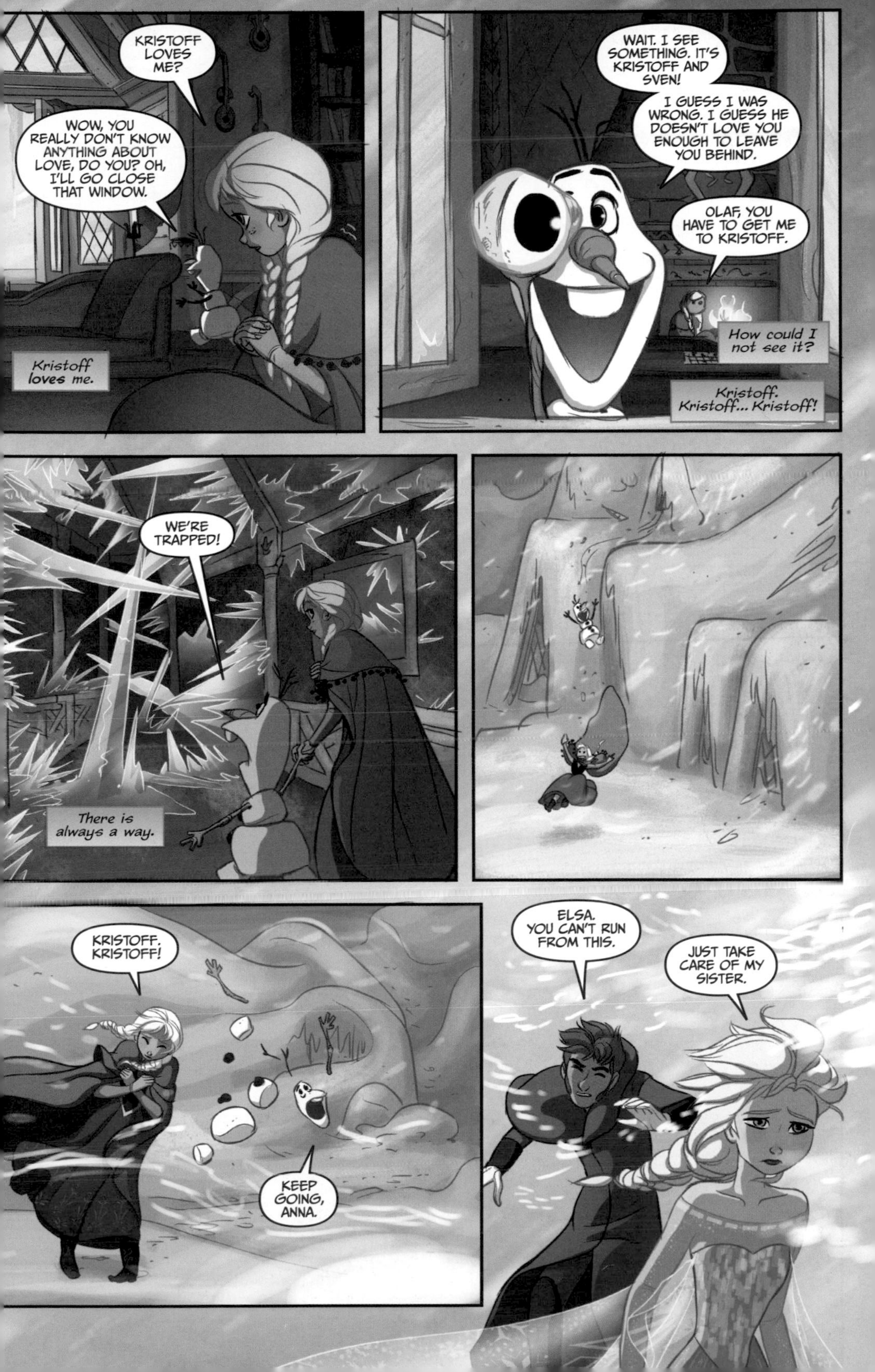
KRISTOFF LOVES ME?
WOW, YOU REALLY DON'T KNOW ANYTHING ABOUT LOVE, DO YOU? OH, I'LL GO CLOSE THAT WINDOW.
Kristoff loves me.
WAIT. I SEE SOMETHING. IT'S KRISTOFF AND SVEN!
I GUESS I WAS WRONG. I GUESS HE DOESN'T LOVE YOU ENOUGH TO LEAVE YOU BEHIND.
OLAF, YOU HAVE TO GET ME TO KRISTOFF.
How could I not see it?
Kristoff. Kristoff... Kristoff!
WE'RE TRAPPED!
There is always a way.
KRISTOFF. KRISTOFF!
KEEP GOING, ANNA.
ELSA. YOU CAN'T RUN FROM THIS.
JUST TAKE CARE OF MY SISTER.

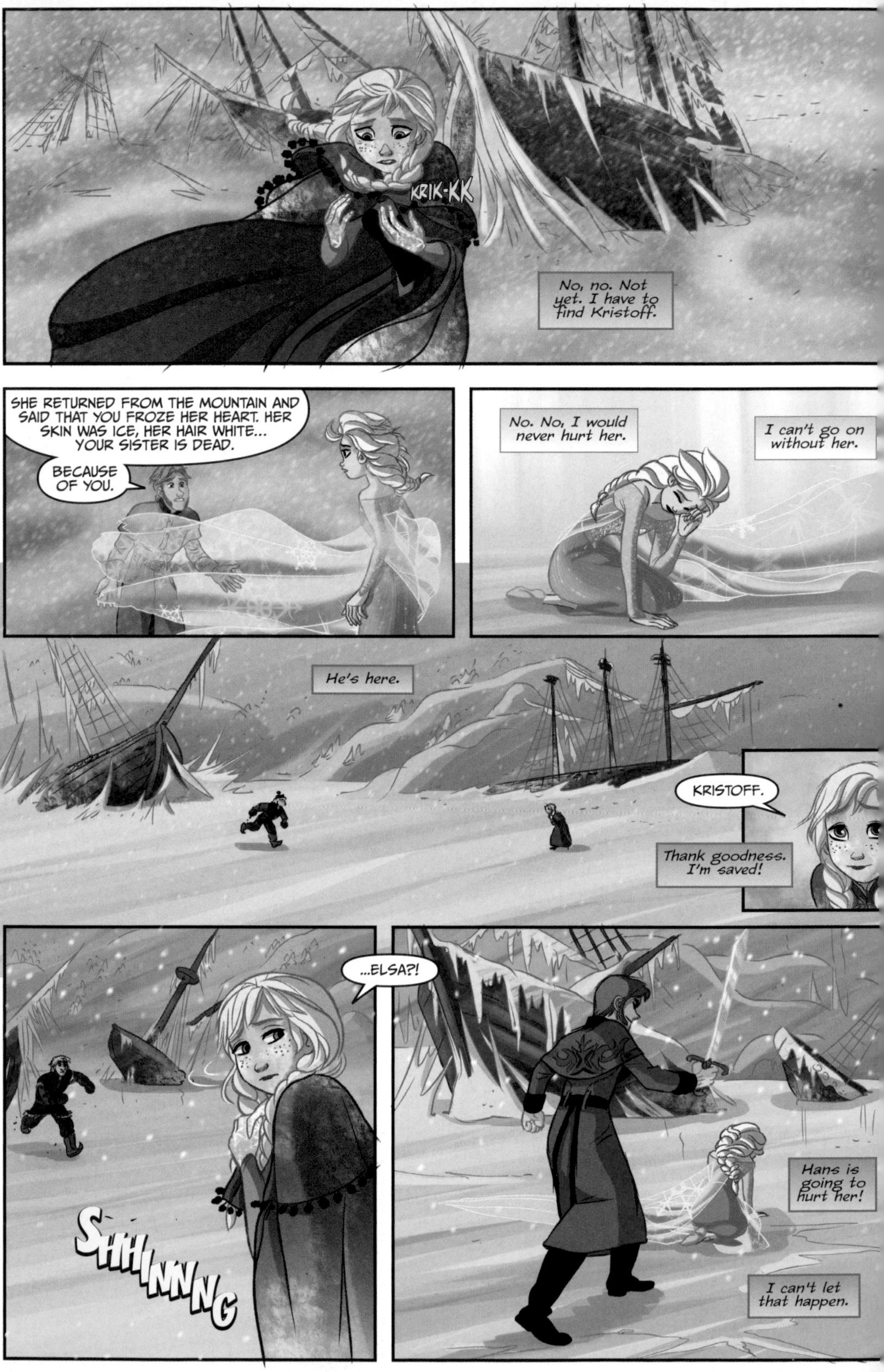
KRIK-KK
No, no. Not yet. I have to find Kristoff.
SHE RETURNED FROM THE MOUNTAIN AND SAID THAT YOU FROZE HER HEART. HER SKIN WAS ICE, HER HAIR WHITE... YOUR SISTER IS DEAD.
BECAUSE OF YOU.
No. No, I would never hurt her.
I can't go on without her.
He's here.
KRISTOFF.
Thank goodness. I'm saved!
...ELSA?!
SHHINNNG
Hans is going to hurt her!
I can't let that happen.

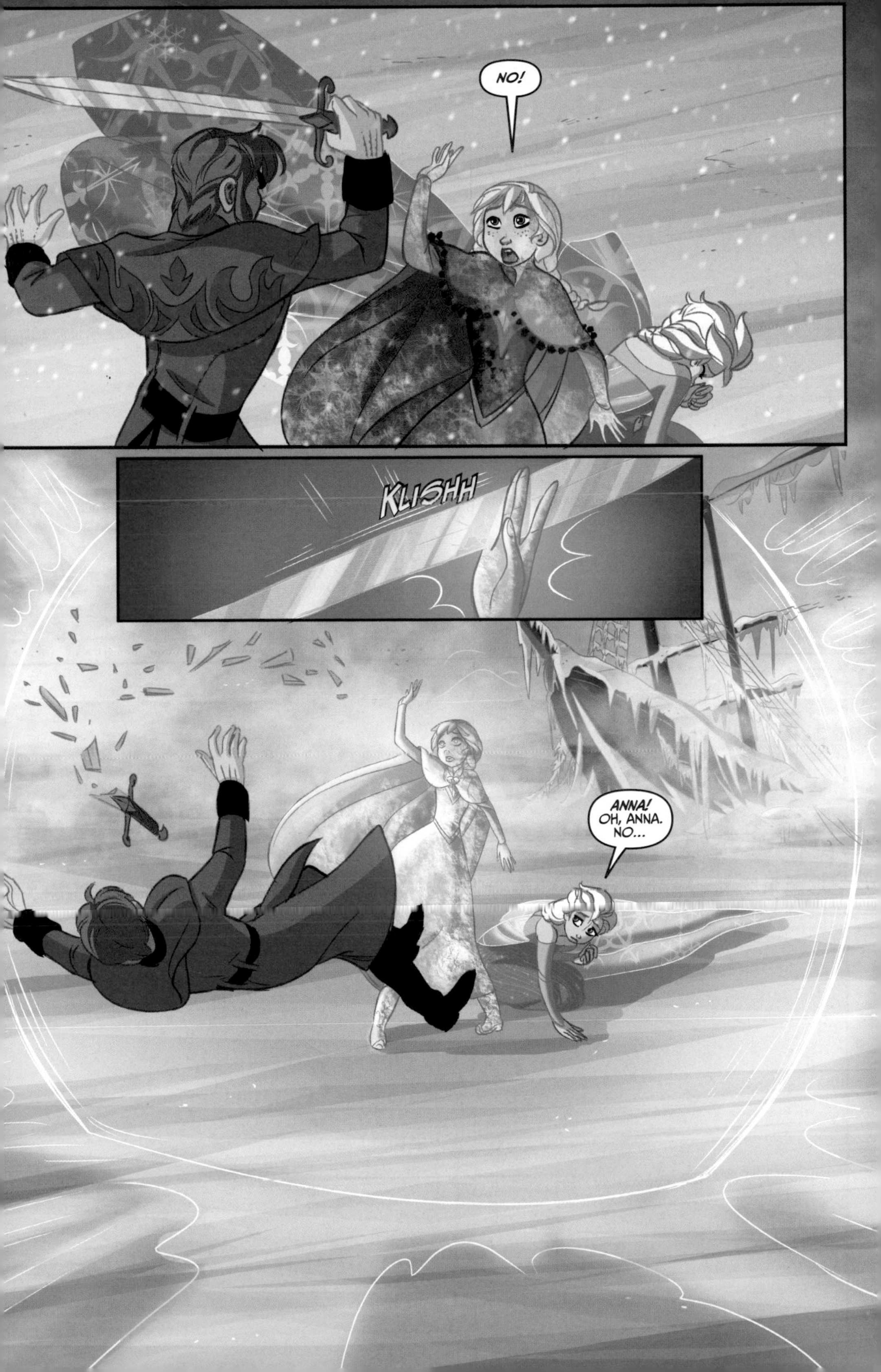
NO!
KLISHH
ANNA! OH, ANNA. NO...

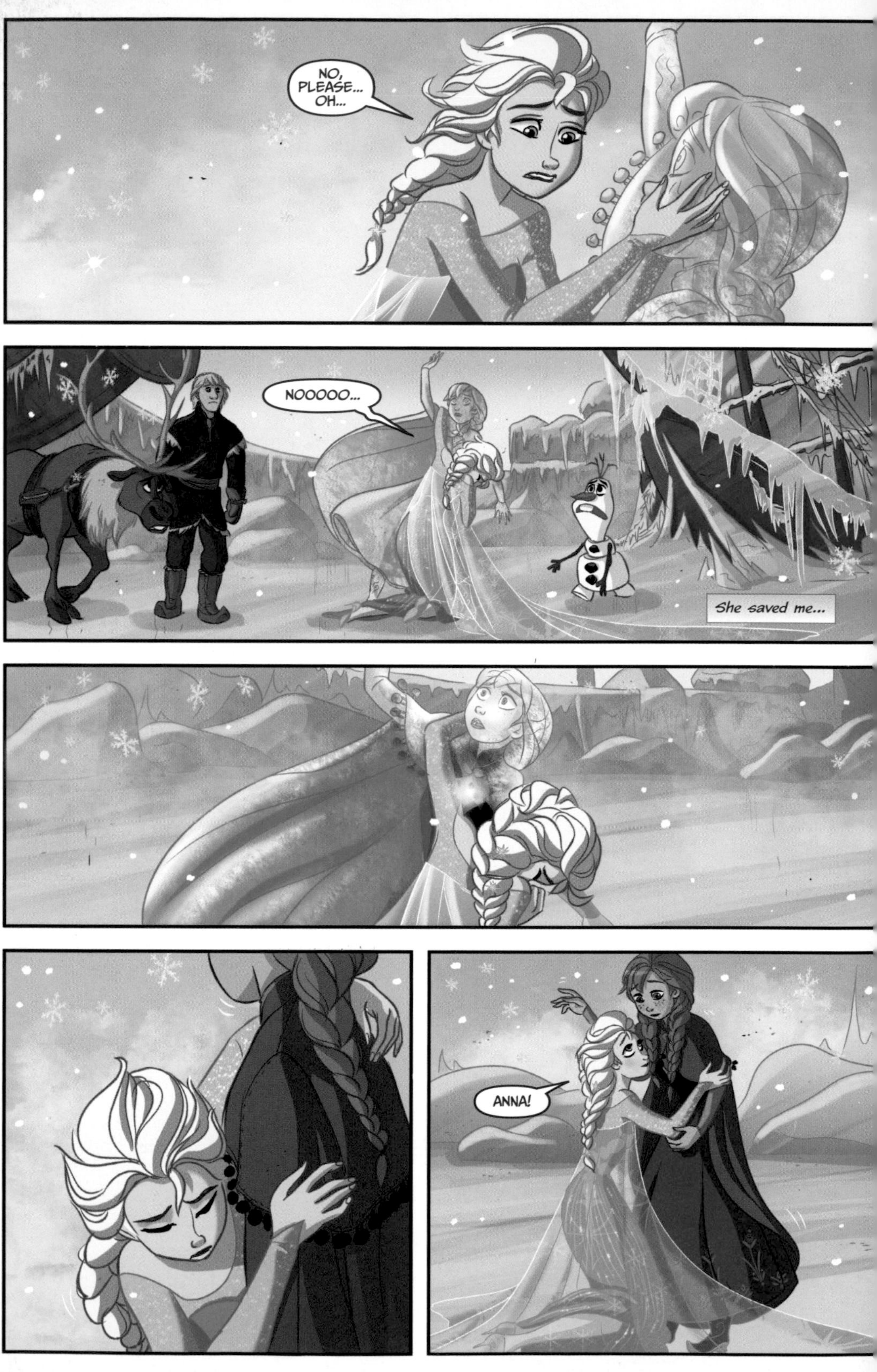
NO, PLEASE... OH...
NOOOOO...
She saved me...
ANNA!

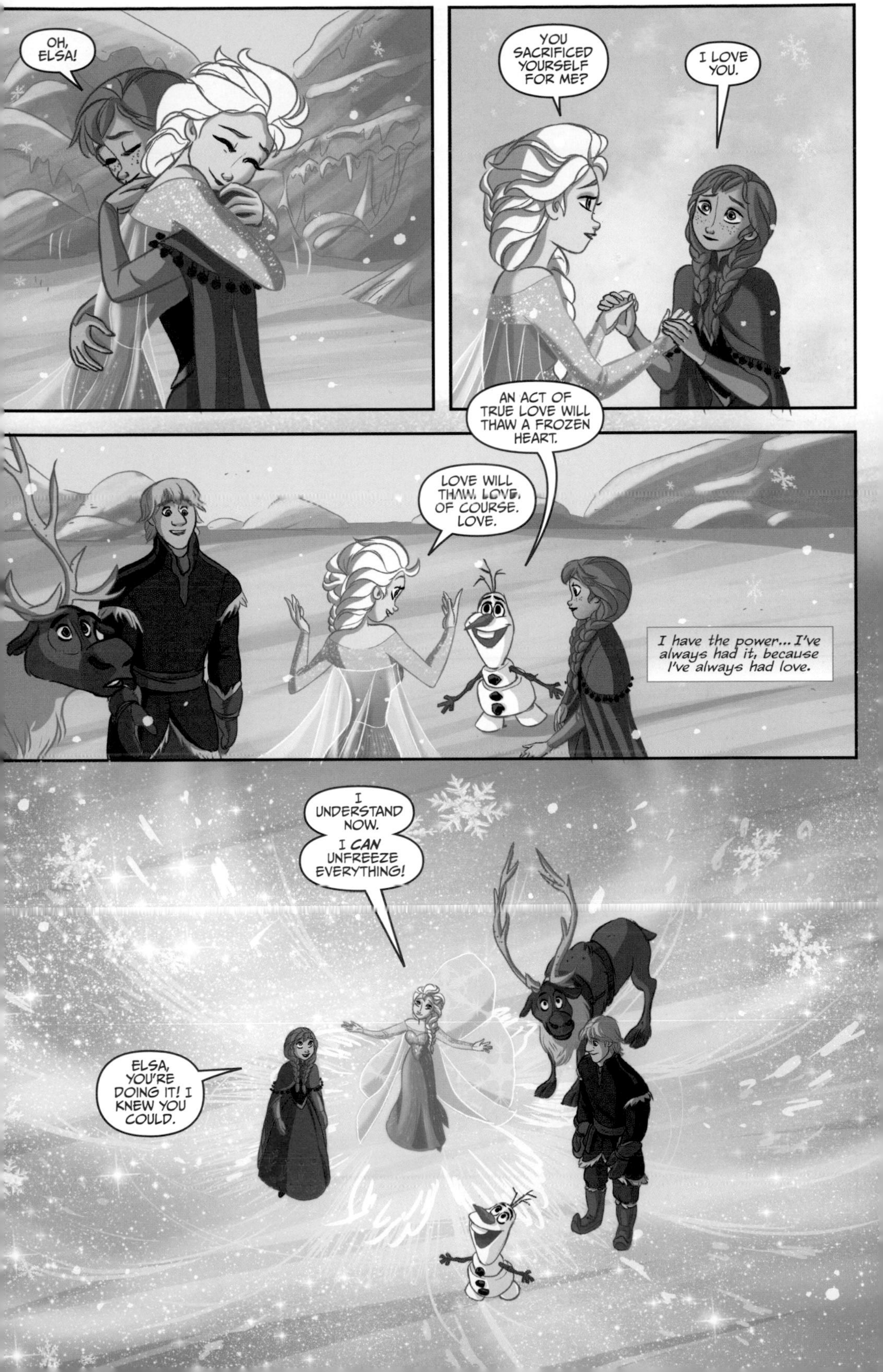

OH, ELSA!
YOU SACRIFICED YOURSELF FOR ME?
I LOVE YOU.
AN ACT OF TRUE LOVE WILL THAW A FROZEN HEART.
LOVE WILL THAW. LOVE. OF COURSE. LOVE.
I have the power... I've always had it, because I've always had love.
I UNDERSTAND NOW.
I *CAN* UNFREEZE EVERYTHING!
ELSA, YOU'RE DOING IT! I KNEW YOU COULD.

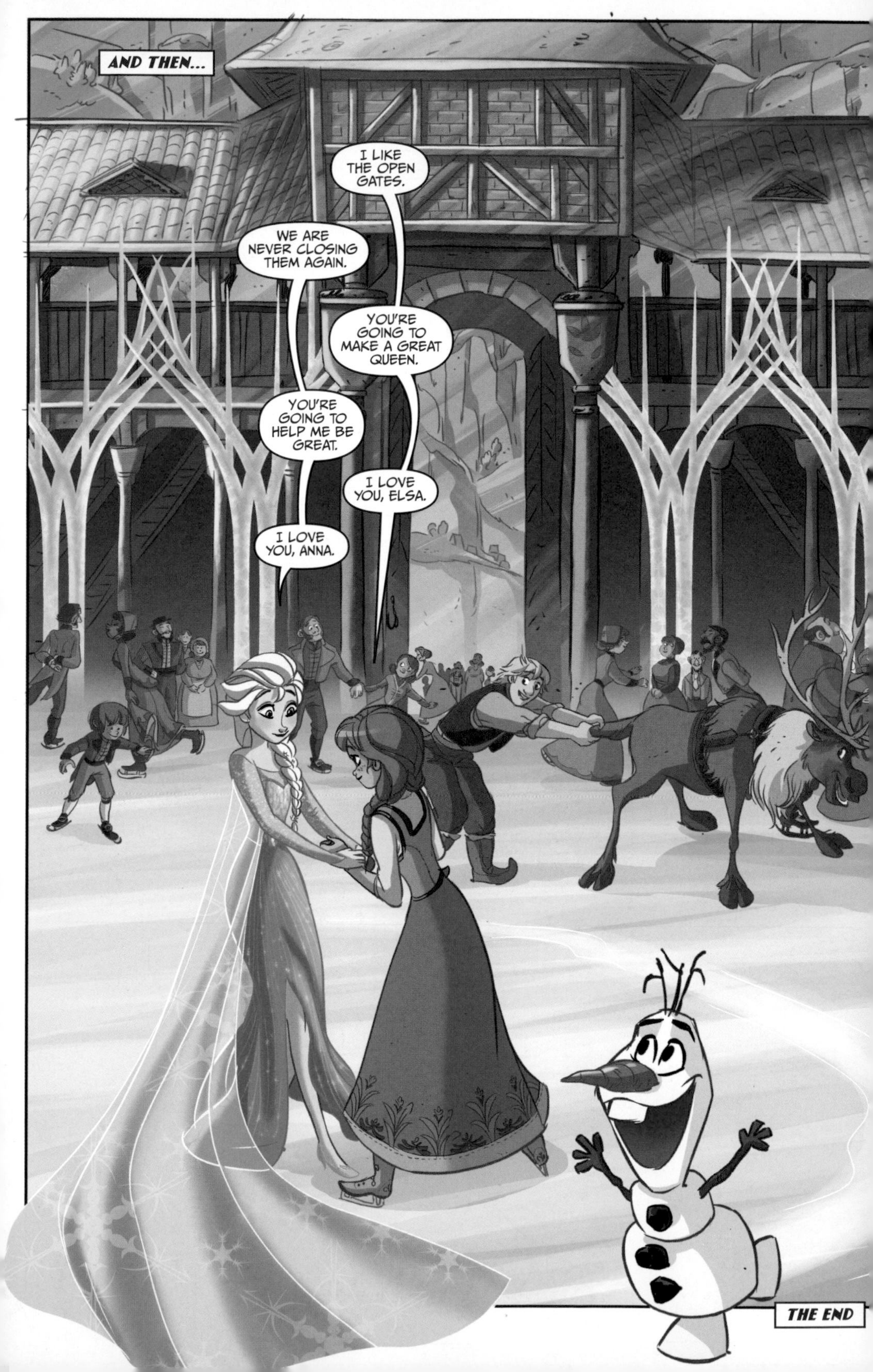
AND THEN...
I LIKE THE OPEN GATES.
WE ARE NEVER CLOSING THEM AGAIN.
YOU'RE GOING TO MAKE A GREAT QUEEN.
YOU'RE GOING TO HELP ME BE GREAT.
I LOVE YOU, ELSA.
I LOVE YOU, ANNA.
THE END

Disney

FROZEN

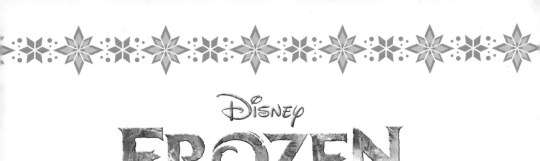

SKETCHBOOK

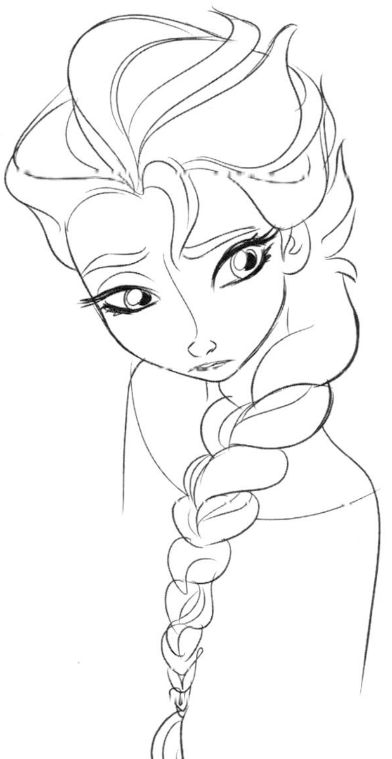

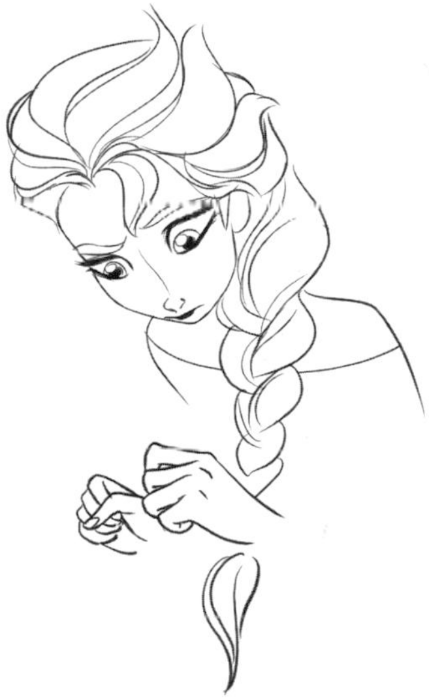

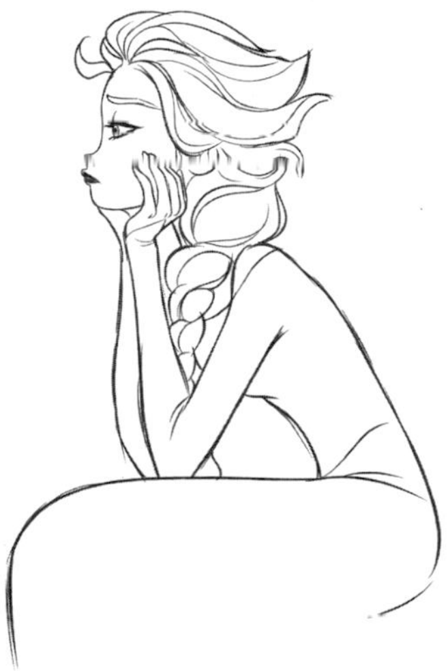

ELSA

Character sketches of Elsa from artist Paola Antista.

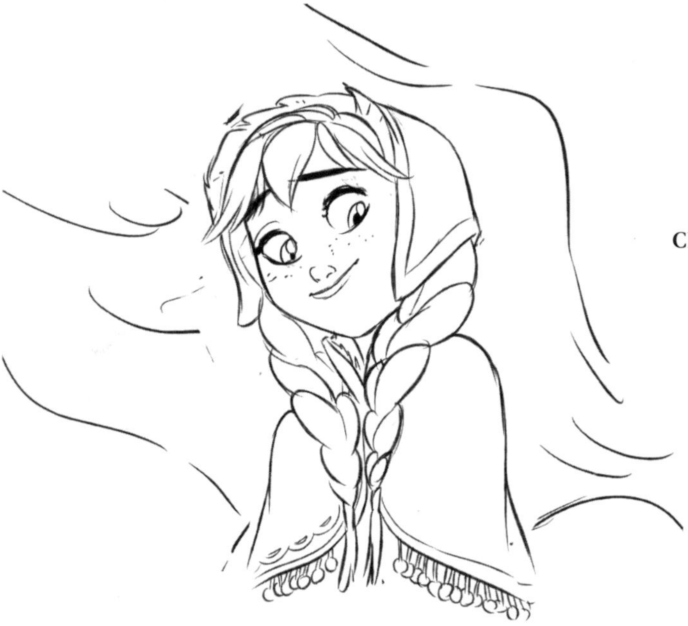

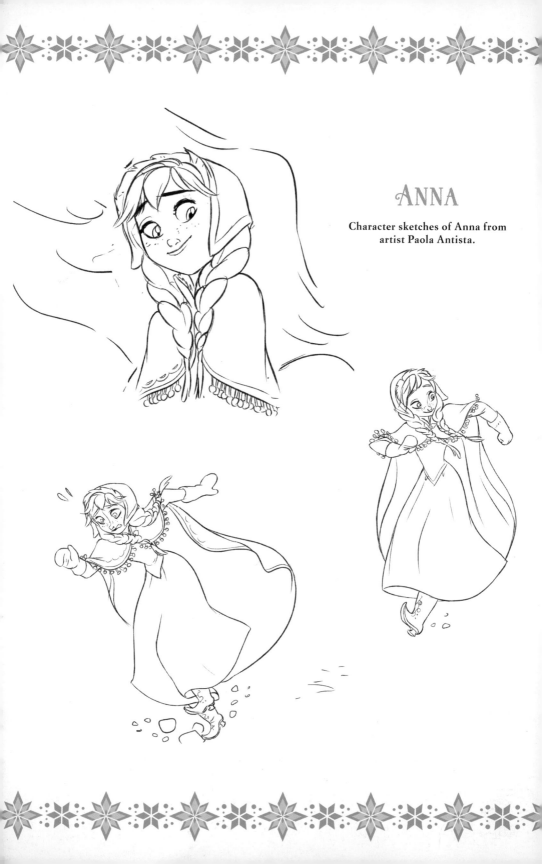

ANNA

Character sketches of Anna from artist Paola Antista.

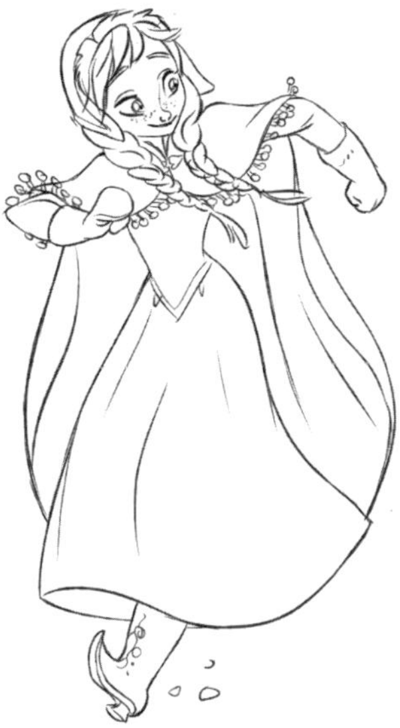

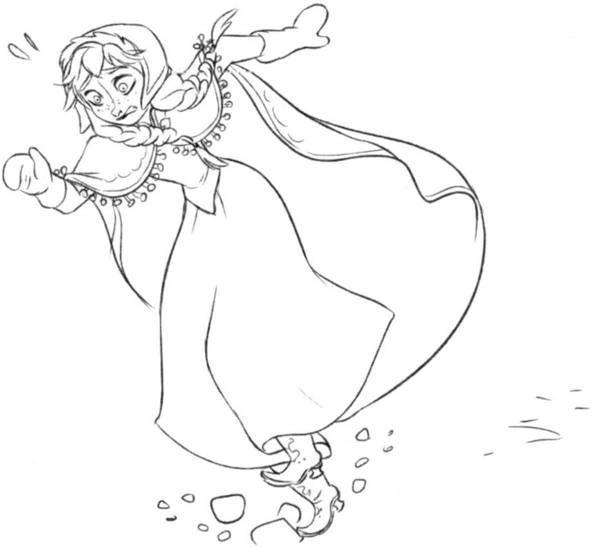

Looking for Disney *Frozen*?
$10.99 each!

Disney Frozen:
Breaking Boundaries
978-1-50671-051-8

Anna, Elsa, and friends have a
quest to fulfill, mysteries to solve,
and peace to restore!

Disney Frozen:
Reunion Road
978-1-50671-270-3

Elsa and Anna gather friends
and family for an unforgettable
trip to a harvest festival in the
neighboring kingdom of Snoob!

Disney Frozen:
The Hero Within
978-1-50671-269-7

Anna, Elsa, Kristoff, Sven, Olaf,
and new friend Hedda, deal with
bullies and the harsh environment
of the Forbidden Land!

Disney Frozen:
True Treasure
978-1-50671-705-0

A lead-in story to Disney
Frozen 2. Elsa and Anna embark
on an adventure searching for
clues to uncover a lost message
from their mother.

Disney Frozen Adventures:
Flurries of Fun
978-1-50671-470-7

Disney Frozen Adventures:
Snowy Stories
978-1-50671-471-4

Disney Frozen Adventures:
Ice and Magic
978-1-50671-472-1

Collections of short comics stories expanding on the world of Disney *Frozen*!

A GRAND ADVENTURE!

From Shuster Award–winning and Eisner–nominated
writer Cecil Castellucci, with art by José Pimenta!

"Castellucci has created a strong heroine who both defies conventionality and embodies empowerment."
—KIRKUS REVIEWS

**Two misfits with no place to call home take a train-hopping journey
from the cold heartbreak of their eastern homes to the sunny promise
of California in this Depression-era coming-of-age tale.**

ISBN 978-1-61655-431-6 · $14.99